CROWN CHEMISTRY

PACIFIC PASSIONS - BOOK TWO

COURTNEY CLARK MICHAELS

AUGUST PUBLISHING

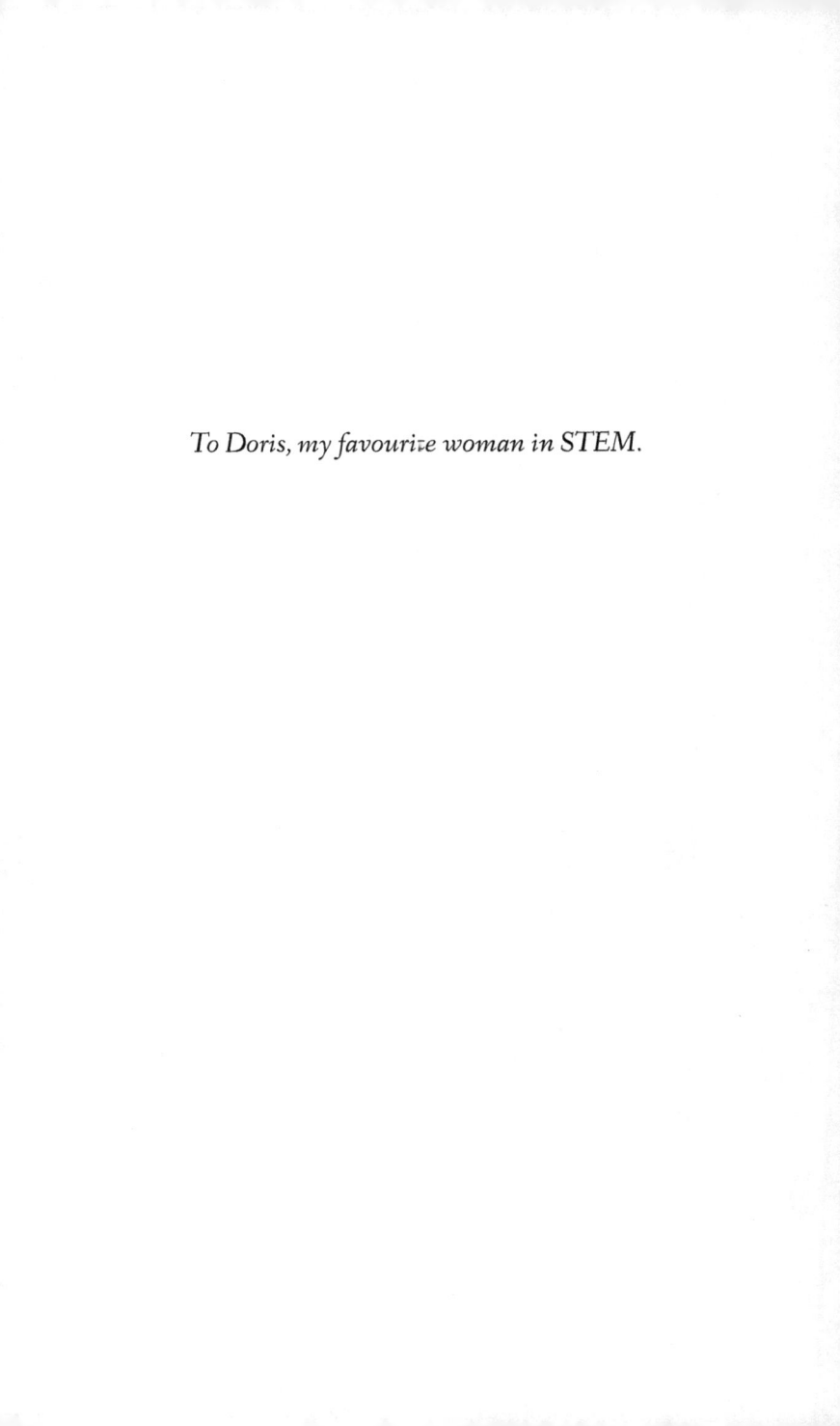

To Doris, my favourite woman in STEM.

CONTENT NOTES

This book contains depiction of the following: off page injury and death in a car accident, main character working in fertility services, and an anxiety attack.

Every effort has been made by the author to handle this content with sensitivity, however please consider this whether this content may be upsetting for you as a reader, and take care of yourself as a reader.

ONE

"But I hate people." Clare Trescott's voice echoed through her living room - her lovely, empty living room - like the bells of war.

"I know you do." The smooth tones of Theo 'Tex' Miller, her former foster brother, current landlord and only true friend, hummed through her phone speaker. "Think of it as a favour to me."

"Letting some random sleep in your bedroom for three months while you're off saving the world is a favour to you?"

"Not technically a random." Tex offered, holding it out like a consolation prize over the phone. "A friend of a friend of a friend. Apparently the place he was supposed to be in fell through. And to be honest—" he hesitated briefly, "—I already said yes. He's supposed to be there around eight tonight. I could use the rent money, Clare."

Clare pulled a face at the phone, secure in the knowledge that Tex was a zillion miles away in some unknown foreign land, doing God-knows-what for the New Zealand Army, while she sat wrapped up in three blankets on his tan leather sectional.

"Fine." She sighed into the phone. The money factor was one she couldn't argue with. Growing up in the system together, both she and Tex had a burning need for financial security. He'd used his military money to put a deposit on the Auckland city flat they shared, and he'd cut her a deal on rent while she'd studied fertility science. Now that she'd worked her way up to be an embryologist in a private clinic in the city she paid her fair share, but she always felt slightly indebted to Tex for the support he'd given her in the early years. "I'll let a stranger move in here. Short term *only*." She stressed the last word, concern that Tex might pull this crap every time he was stationed overseas creeping in.

"And you'll be nice?"

"I'm always nice."

A snort echoed down the phone, matching her own as they sniggered together over her blatant lie.

"I'll be as nice as I can," Clare amended, as she fiddled with the silver St Christopher's necklace Tex had given her for her twenty-first birthday.

"I appreciate it, Clare Bear. You're the best."

"No, you are." She sighed down the phone again. "I'll talk to you later. Stay safe."

"You too, Clare Bear. Nighty night."

Clare thumbed off her phone and tossed it further down the couch, before exhaling heavily as she glanced around the open-plan kitchen and living area. She loved this apartment - like *love, loved* it - and the idea of sharing her personal space for the first time in a decade with anyone who wasn't Tex niggled at her like a thorn in her side.

Eighteen years in the foster care system had bred a natural wariness into her. Having never been adopted, she'd come across all sorts in her journey - she'd been burgled, spat on and verbally abused by both the parents and kids who'd claimed to want to care for her over the years. That was why Tex's small two-bedroom flat, with its big caramel couch, plain white walls and bulbous hanging copper light shades, felt like such a haven. She never had to worry when she was here. Bringing someone else into their sanctuary was a risk she wouldn't have taken voluntarily, but it wasn't her call. If Tex said he needed rent money, then he needed it. And she would never deny Tex something he needed.

Clare checked her watch. *Seven pm. Plenty of time for dinner.* She hefted a chunky cream blanket off her and stood, stretching towards the ceiling as high as her five foot four frame could reach, and then she sank forward into a toe-touch. Energy zinged through her legs and up her torso as the muscles lengthened. Straightening, she headed down the hall to the apartment entrance and grabbed her cheery yellow coat off the hook by the door and her e-reader off the table under it. Skipping the lift, she bounced down five flights of stairs, out the glass doors and into the pub on the corner.

"Hey, Clare," Cole the Bartender greeted her. "The usual?"

"The usual." She headed to the back booth, empty as it always was on a Tuesday night, chucked her coat onto the burgundy velour and slid in beside it, powering on her e-reader.

Bliss.

Tuesdays at the pub were her ritual. A steak meal and raspberry fizzy drink, with a few chapters to read while she waited. No phone, no distractions, just satisfying food for her belly and her brain. Tuesdays were the only weeknight she didn't stay at work past five reading up on conception rates and genome testing. The world of fertility science was fast-paced, and if she wanted a promotion to Laboratory

Manager, she needed to keep on top of any rapid developments that could be useful in the New Zealand market.

Tex joined her for her weekly meal when he was in town, and over the last few years, she'd become enough of a regular that she'd seen Cole the Bartender go from a skinny kid fresh from high school to a married man with a child of his own.

She'd just gotten comfortable when there was a thunk and a literal god sat down across from her in the booth, grinning at her over a pint of amber beer.

"Hey there."

Clare stared at him, positive the horror coursing through her system was readable on her face. Not only was he *in her Tuesday booth*, but he was quite possibly the most attractive man she'd ever laid eyes on.

Warm brown eyes, crinkled at the corner like they were sharing a joke, danced out at her from the dark skin of his face. His features were all large - a wide nose and full lips framed by a strong jaw and high forehead. A single dimple creased his left cheek. His long hair was pulled back from his face and lay in two tidy braids across shoulders that looked like they could be used for transporting a busload of small children to safety in the event of a flood. Not unlike the sudden one in her pants.

Still smiling at her, he cocked an eyebrow. Awareness that she was staring like a moron drifted through her, slow at first, then speeding up until the hot flush of embarrassment slid up her neck.

"Can I help you?"

"I'm killing time until an appointment. Do you mind if I sit here?"

"Yes," Clare replied bluntly, but the Stranger God just laughed and nodded towards her e-reader.

"What are you reading about?"

"Venereal diseases." It was true. She was reading the biography of Ettie Rout, a New Zealand nurse famous for working to protect soldiers from sexually transmitted diseases during World War One.

The Stranger God's thick eyebrows shot up.

"Do you have one?"

"Go away."

He laughed again, a deep, rich sound with the hint of an accent that reached inside her and twisted. She shook her head as though she could mentally bat away the glow in her chest at his attention and refocused on her screen.

A beat. Then ...

"I'm thinking about getting one of those. Do you reckon they're better than actual books?"

Clare sighed heavily. First, Tex letting a stranger move into the apartment, and now this. Was there no end to her torment today? Very deliberately, she powered off the device, flipped the cover closed and placed it on the polished wood of the table. She raised her eyes to the Stranger God's, ignoring the frisson of awareness that ran straight from her nipples to her underwear, and enunciated clearly.

"What. Do. You. Want?"

"I'd like to take you out sometime. If that's not an option, I'd like to chat to you now while I wait."

"No."

"No?"

"You heard me." She narrowed her eyes, pinning him with Death Glare Number Two. "I'm here alone, and I don't want company. In a minute, I'm going to eat the best steak in the central city, finish a single chapter of my book, then go home and put on flannel pyjamas. This is my only night off. I have no desire to sit here stroking your ego while you hope you're charming enough to talk me into stroking something else. It's not going to happen. Please leave me alone."

His surprised gaze roamed over her face, and for a second, she thought she was going to have to upgrade to Death Glare Number Three, but he nodded and slid out of the booth.

"I'm sorry to have disturbed you, miss. My apologies. Please enjoy your evening."

He gave a funny little bow motion and wandered back towards the bar just as Cole the Bartender rounded it with her meal and walked over to set the plate in front of her.

She did a happy little dance in her seat at the sight of the juicy steak piled high atop a stack of thick, golden chips and the side salad peeking around from the back. Still, even as she sank her knife through beef that parted like butter, a feeling of being watched niggled at the base of her spine. It lingered throughout her meal, seasoning the flavour of the food, but every time she snuck a look at the bar, where the only other patron sat, the Stranger God and Cole the Bartender were engaged in a lively debate about some kind of sport being shown on the telly above the rows of gleaming bottles.

When frustration over her inability to concentrate on her book finally edged out the stubbornness that had kept her trying for a full half hour after she'd cleaned her plate, she stood. Shoving her fists through the arms of her yellow coat, she headed towards the bar, where Cole the Bartender now leaned alone, despite the inexplicable presence of a suitcase by the register.

"All done?"

"All done." She fished in her coat pocket for her card, but he shook his head.

"No need. Your mate took care of it."

Shock coursed through Clare. "The human mountain paid for my dinner?"

"That's the one."

"But ..." She floundered. "I don't want him to."

"Too late. You can go wait for him outside the toilets if you want to argue with him about it. But Amanda keeps reminding me that the world is hard enough for women. Take your free meals where you can get them."

"There's no such thing as a free meal," Clare intoned darkly, pulling her brows together.

"Well, you and my lovely wife can debate that point in your own time. For now, your tab is clear."

"But—"

"Clare." He interrupted with exaggerated patience. "Do you have any idea how much that man makes?"

Confusion tripped through her. What had Cole the Bartender done? Run a credit check on his customer? Did the Stranger God have one of those fancy bank cards with 'Esquire' stamped on it? She hadn't taken him for the sort who cared about a person's wealth.

"No?"

Cole the Bartender laughed. "Trust me. Your steak isn't going to make a dent. Will I see you tomorrow?"

Clare snorted in response. He'd been trying to get her to the pub on Wednesdays for the best part of two years.

"Not a chance, Cole the Bartender. See you next week."

MANU STOOD outside the apartment building in the thick blanket of night, his breath visible in the crisp air as he looked up at the lit windows peeking through the darkness like stars.

How has it come to this? Dropped mid-season from his club, only to be picked up by one of the worst teams in the competition, and living with a stranger because all of the team's accommodations were already in use. He was Manu Esera, for Christ's sake. Maybe that didn't carry as much weight as it used to, but it was nothing to sneeze at. He was a prince. A professional athlete. He was listed in the Top Ten Most Bangable Stars of Rugby League. Which, unfortunately, differed greatly from the Top Ten Most Bankable Stars, but still wasn't anything to complain about. Yet here he was, shunned and shivering, not even able to tempt a girl into a date anymore. Huffing out a sigh, he pressed the buzzer for apartment 5A.

After what seemed like an eternity standing on the city street holding a suitcase that contained the essentials of his world, the lock on the glass door clicked, and he pushed through into the cool, tiled interior. The chill only intensified as he stepped out of the lift on the fifth floor and knocked on the door marked 5A. His light training shorts and an old Giants hoodie had seemed enough on the plane over from Australia, but he was beginning to suspect his usual clothing choices wouldn't be a match for an Auckland winter.

And then the door to 5A opened and the temperature ratcheted up about a thousand degrees as he took in the sight in front of him. It was the girl from the bar. Black hair, huge grey eyes, and a lush mouth made for sin. Abundant curves clothed in black. Betty Boop Goes Goth. Arousal socked him in the gut, fizzing through his blood and waking up nerve endings that had been missing in action since he'd been dropped from the Giants. The fact she was glaring at him barely registered.

"What do you want now?" The words were clipped, irritated. As though he'd knocked on her door just to offer her the Good Word of Jesus Christ, despite the suitcase at his hip and the emailed assurance from the apartment's owner that he was expected.

"I'm Manu." He waited.

Nothing.

"I'm supposed to be renting a room in this apartment. Fully furnished? The guy who usually has it is overseas?"

Her eyes skipped over him, quick and perfunctory, no lingering. She frowned, her full lips curving in a scowl, and a bolt of lust seared towards his groin.

You absolute sicko, Esera.

The angry-looking china doll in front of him opened the door wider and then turned and walked back into the apartment, muttering to herself. Manu was pretty sure he caught the phrase 'bloody army boys'."

Taking it as all the invitation he was going to get - and technically she was being *paid* for this - he kicked his shoes off and traversed the pale wooden hallway her truly luscious ass had disappeared down, walking past a series of hooks all hung with different coloured jackets and rolling his suitcase behind him.

He found her in an open-plan kitchen and living area staring into the fridge.

She glanced up and noticed him, and he could have sworn her eyes rolled, just a little.

"I'm not in the army," he offered, because it seemed as good a place to start as any.

Her wide eyes expanded even further with horror. "You do *have* a job, don't you?"

"Yes, I have a job." His voice tightened with irritation. "I'm a professional rugby league player."

Her aghast expression increased.

"Lord help me," she muttered under her breath. "Okay." Her voice was clearer now, taking up more of the space. "It's a pretty basic place." She shut the refrigerator door and waved an arm around. He caught a flash of turquoise fingernails. "Kitchen and living room here, balcony out the glass door over there. Bathroom and bedrooms are back down the hall; your room is the closest to the front door. Washing machine and dryer are hidden in a cupboard on the right back down the hall. Any questions?"

He shook his head and the obstinate set of her jaw softened slightly.

"I'm Clare-without-an-i," his reluctant flatmate offered. "Do you want a coffee?" She gestured to the capsule coffee maker on the white granite-look bench beside her.

"Can you do a mocha?"

"A mocha?"

"Yeah." Manu shifted from side to side, a buzz of discomfort fluttering over his skin as she continued to stare at him without moving. "Y'know, a cappuccino with chocolate?"

"I know what a mocha is."

"That's, um ... that's what I drink."

"Okay then." Clare-without-an-i turned towards the coffee maker and Manu escaped back down the hallway. He pushed open the last door before the entrance and pleasurable surprise soaked through him. The streetlight outside bathed the west-facing room in a pool of golden light that spilled over the plain grey duvet and neatly turned-down navy top-sheet. The room was clean and sparsely decorated - a generic oak bedhead, one plain grey nightstand, a large corner desk with an excessive number of power points surrounding it, and a wall of mirrors that slid open to reveal a wardrobe with built-in shelving. Not the greatest place he'd ever lived in - though being raised in a palace, even one in a little-known Pacific Islands nation, set a high standard - but certainly not the worst.

He set his suitcase down on its side and flipped the combo lock to open it. A tangle of sports gear swarmed out as soon as the lid opened, creeping halfway across the floor in a mess of mesh and moisture-wicking fabrics. A pang of regret passed through him at the lack of formalwear. He loved clothes. The colours, the fabrics, the weight and fit and cut of a beautiful piece of clothing, whether Pacific or Western in style. He'd left all but one basic suit-and-tie combo at home in Avali, and he'd done so on purpose. He was here to play, not to party. He'd play his guts out - run the ball as straight as he could, as hard as he could, as often as he could - until another club came calling and picked him up out of the sporting hellscape that was the Auckland Knights.

There was a knock at the door, and he turned to see Clare holding a chunky white ceramic mug against the dark drape of her black top and jeans, like a domesticated Batman. The aroma of coffee danced towards him and he pulled it into his lungs greedily.

My precious.

"Your mocha."

He reached out a hand, but she sidestepped him neatly and placed the mug on the desk. Avoiding his eyes, she fished a folded slip of paper from her pocket and placed it next to the mug.

"That's the wifi code and the Netflix password. You're welcome to read any of the books in the lounge. We do groceries separately, and I'll let you know when the bills come in so you can pay half."

"The club takes care of that." He kept his voice gentle. The way her gaze was flickering all over the room hinted that she was close to flight. But at his words, her head jerked back like she'd been mildly electrocuted, and she stared at him in blatant disbelief.

"Your job pays your bills?"

"Yeah." He shrugged off the prickle of her judgement before it became a sting. He couldn't help the benefits of his job. "It's part of the contract. I should be in one of their own facilities right now, but I'm a late signing and they were all allocated at the beginning of the season, so someone tracked this place down."

Disdain was still radiating off her in waves, so he changed the topic. "What do you do?"

"I'm a scientist."

Ah. That explains a lot, then.

Manu's experiences with women since he'd first been scouted as a potential player of interest in the Under 16's had fallen into exactly two categories. First, women who wanted to sleep with him. Admittedly, the fact he was a prince might have had something to do with that too, but the offers had become more blatant once the training jerseys settled into his wardrobe. Second, women who did not want to sleep with him. Women who were decidedly unimpressed with his choice in career. And, rightly or not, Manu had often surmised that these women tended to have careers in academic fields. Not that it bothered him. The options in the first category were numerous enough to make up for any rejection from those in the second, no matter how little he took them up on their offers.

But, for some reason, discomfort itched under his skin at the idea that Clare might fall into the second category. It wasn't like he was ever going to have sex with her, no matter how much the ache in his groin protested that claim. Even if it weren't for his personal circumstances, they were living together and that was a recipe for disaster. But he wasn't used to it, this uncertainty that wrapped itself round him like tendrils at the idea that he might finally have met a woman he wanted more than she wanted him.

TWO

The senior conference room of North Hope Fertility Centre was buzzing with Monday morning chatter as scientists, doctors, nurses and administrative employees piled into the room for their weekly meeting. Clare sat in one of the plush navy chairs at the end of the long table nursing a steaming black coffee and letting the noise wash over her. She was still fizzing with an annoying combination of indignation and lust from seeing Manu in the kitchen this morning. She'd been minding her own business, filling her reusable water bottle, when he'd strolled in *sweating,* despite it only being seven in the morning, with his thick hair pulled back from his face in two long braids and grinned at her. *Grinned!* As though seeing her with a rat's nest of hair, in slouchy socks and an oversized t-shirt that said 'Stand back, I'm about to science the shit out of this' was somehow a delightful surprise and not a gross intrusion of her privacy.

I hope Tex is mildly wounded. Perhaps a non-poisonous snake bite, or a pulled groin muscle that makes it impossible for him to masturbate.

Her vicious revenge fantasies on her best friend for putting her in such an uncomfortable living situation were quickly dismissed as the chair next to her was pulled out and a giant lumberjack settled next to her.

"Good morning, Clare."

"Jeremy." The new team leader seemed unnaturally nice, and was also a clear threat to her dreams of becoming lab manager, so Clare had made a special effort not to be too friendly towards him, despite his daily desire to engage her in meaningless chit chat. She also had severe reservations about the health and safety aspects of his ginger beard.

"How was your night?"

"Fine."

"Mine too." Jeremy momentarily dazzled her with a smile that should be selling toothpaste the world over and took advantage of her stunned silence as she blinked away the white spots dancing in her eyes to press on. "What was the most exciting thing that happened to you during it?"

Is he kidding?

"I got a new flatmate." Clare kept her voice as bland as possible.

"Ooh, anyone nice?" Jeremy waggled his eyebrows at her, the two little miniature dachshunds on his forehead dancing up and down like puppets on speed.

"No."

"Well, I'm sure they'll be lovely. They couldn't possibly live with someone as delightful as you and not have it rub off on them."

She glared at Jeremy until his smirk dropped and he looked away. It coincided nicely with their current lab manager, Trish, shuffling papers at the head of the table and clearing her throat for attention.

"Right." Trish was a tiny Korean-New Zealand

dynamo who ran the centre like a foul-mouthed Napoleon. Clare loved her. "Shitloads of patients through today. Every single team is doing at least four implantations, so make sure you're running to schedule so the doctors don't get backed up. Team leaders, keep your communication clear." Clare nodded quickly, along with Jeremy next to her and their fellow team leaders Hilary and James across the table, as Trish ran her narrow gaze over them all before continuing. "Don't forget your performance reviews today either. Nurses, we're in the process of moving the semen vials out of Tank Four, so today's collections will have to move to the back row as soon as they're processed. Any questions, see me." Trish glanced around the room quickly. "Alright, everyone. Go make dreams come true."

Clare was out of her seat before the lab manager could finish stalking from the room.

"Trish?"

"Ah, Clare." Trish didn't even slow down. "Walk and talk. What do you need?"

"I've got the first performance review today."

"Yes."

"Can we do it now? I wanted to go over the new roster system with my nurses before clients come in."

Trish paused outside her office and ran her gaze over Clare.

"Fine. Come in."

She followed Trish into the spacious office and sat carefully on one of the sleek white chairs in front of the glass-and-steel desk, hoping she wasn't shedding any leftover breakfast croissant crumbs.

Trish pulled a red folder labelled with Clare's name from a neat stack on one side of her desk and placed it in the middle of the table. She didn't open it, merely looked over it at Clare.

"You know I'm moving on before the end of the year?"

Anticipation rose in Clare. "I'm aware."

"Will you be applying for my position?"

"Yes."

Please let me get it, please let me get it.

"Why do you want it?"

The question caught Clare off guard and she stumbled.

"Uh, I ... well, uh. The opportunity for growth, obviously. Increased responsibility—" *increased pay* "—and being able to have a say in the hiring processes to ensure the highest standard of staff."

Trish leaned back in her giant ergonomic chair, looking every inch a queen in her flowing white blouse in front of neatly filed folders and a giant piece of modern art in violent red slashes that Clare found vaguely horrifying.

"I'm going to give it to you straight, because I know you can take it. Your science is A plus. Can't fault it. Clear and thorough analysis through the testing stages, strong creation work, great results with implantation. But this position isn't about the science. It's about the people."

Anger slid through Clare, clicking into place in her chest as Trish's meaning took hold.

"Science isn't a popularity contest."

"No. But management can be." Trish paused for a moment, assessing her. "People don't like you, Clare. You're blunt. You rub some of the patients the wrong way. Hell, you rub some of the *staff* the wrong way. This is an emotional job. People are often at their lowest point when they come to us. Yes, dreams come true in this building, but they die here too. That affects everyone."

"I know that." Clare made a concerted effort to gentle

the natural snap of her voice, to sound compassionate even as irritation bubbled under her skin. "I am a professional, and I ensure all my patients feel their needs have been met, regardless of the outcome."

Trish shrugged and pushed the folder in front of her across the desk with one perfect black fingernail.

Huffing, Clare picked it up and flicked through the pages. Her lab results were there, as positive as one could get in the game of life, evidence of her ongoing professional development and published work, and at the back, patient satisfaction surveys. She skimmed over them, her eyes picking out the words that seemed to be repeated on almost every page.

Cold. Standoffish. Uncaring.

"I'm not uncaring." She looked up at Trish, whose mouth was twisted in knowing sympathy.

"No?"

"I care very much about whether the procedures are successful," Clare responded, striving for calmness and sounding like a robot instead. *There goes that.*

"But do you care about the people undergoing the procedures? Their feelings? How the outcomes affect them beyond the results of the pregnancy test?"

Clare gritted her teeth and said nothing.

Trish nodded slowly. "Look." Her voice was gentle. "There's four months until I leave. Six weeks until applications open. You're a fast learner. You can learn this. And you need to if you want to be in the running for this position."

Clare nodded, her jaw still working in minute move-ments. She thanked Trish tightly and left the office with her mind whirring.

Fuck, fuck, fuckity fuck.

It was slipping away, the silky threads of her dream escaping her grasp on the miserable back of grumblings from patients whose embryos hadn't stuck. And now she had to do what? Go and learn how to be nice? Was there a niceness academy somewhere, full of simpering idiots who spewed sunshine and rainbows? There would definitely be online tutorials. The internet was made for that shit.

"How did it go?"

Clare's head snapped up. James was lounging against the hallway wall, arms folded. She let her face fall back into its natural scowl. James was another of the clinic's team leaders. He looked like a young Marlon Brando and acted like a smug prick.

"Fine." She wasn't in the mood to watch him gloat over her poor review. She'd never be in the mood for that.

"Glowing report?"

She stiffened. "I'm very happy with my work."

He laughed, and it scraped across her nerves like steel wool.

"It's not really about whether you're happy though, is it? It's about whether Trish is." With a smarmy smile painted across his face, he pushed off the wall and stepped past her.

"Wish me luck."

"I wish you crabs." But she said it under her breath. *Progress already.*

THE FAMILIAR SCENT hit Manu as soon as he stepped into the training facility. A heady combination of grass, sweat, leather and liniment. That was the difference right there, between the field and the front office. All the time he and his agent had spent on the phone and in meetings had been to get him here. The Auckland Knights might be a terrible team, trailing towards the bottom of the table, but Manu's focus since the Giants had released him had been getting back to a top-eight team. If he had to do some time in a Knights' jersey to get there, so be it.

"Oi, new kid." The call rang up through the high ceilings.

Manu's clenched his jaw as he turned a slow one-eighty. Finn Chalmers, the Knights' dirty blond fullback, jogged towards him. Scenes from their last few games playing each other flashed in front of Manu. Chalmers had been on the receiving end of more than one of Manu's bone-crunching tackles, but he'd also run two tries over in their last three matchups due to tricky footwork and excellent ball handling. There was also a dubious hair-pulling incident Manu would write off as accidental until he had further evidence.

"Chalmers." He acknowledged the other man with a head tilt as Finn slowed to a stop beside him.

"Hey, Esera. Welcome to the team." Finn clapped a big hand on Manu's shoulder and swung into step beside him as he continued into the building.

A non-committal sound dragged out of Manu's throat. He couldn't say he was pleased to be here because it would be a blatant lie and he tried quite hard to be honest. But nobody could possibly be pleased about being dropped from a team that had made it to the final rounds of the competition in the last four seasons to a team that hadn't seen the inside of a quarter-finals changing shed in over a decade. Instead, he trailed after Chalmers, nodding silently as the other man pointed out the doors to the gym, the indoor running track, pool, sauna and cryotherapy tanks, and the theatre for reviewing game footage.

Chalmers pushed open the door to the team's dressing room and the sound came at him like a wall - raucous laughter and shit talk. The sound of professional sports.

Men milled around in variations of the training gear in the team colours of black and red, tattoos and testosterone on full display as they prepared for the practice ahead. Manu kept his head down searching for his name as he moved around the lockers that surrounded the open space where most of the team were congregated. He found it finally, slashed in marker on a piece of tape on a locker door at the far edges of the room. The impermanence of the gesture lit a spark inside him. The Knights might have picked him up until the end of next year's season, but hope fizzed through him that the temporary naming job indicated they were as uninterested in a long-term commitment as he was.

"*Men!*" The voice cracked through the high-ceilinged space like a whip just as he slung his training bag onto the bench below his locker.

Turning, Manu saw the formidable form of Brian Harrington, flanked on each side by suited soldiers. Harro had been one of the best in the game in his time, known throughout the sport as a man who would worry you to the ground if the first tackle didn't knock you on your arse. Manu played prop, the same position Harro had, and the memory of his bare feet on the hard, sunbaked earth of the island's training ground, as he weaved in and out of the other kids pretending he was the older man, rang through him vividly. Even now, pushing fifty, Harro looked like he wouldn't be opposed to taking the ball up the line himself if he felt he could do a better job. He was still an imposing figure, wide-chested and muscular, between the lean figures of the front office staff who stood alongside him.

"We've got a player joining our ranks today. I'm sure you're all familiar with Manu Esera." The snickers and small grumbles were cut off as Harro continued. "He's a Knight now, so make sure he bloody feels like one. Make him feel welcome and leave any shit you've got from the last game behind."

There was a general murmur of assent and a couple of the guys gave him amiable slaps on the back. The tension leaked out of Manu's body as Harro moved on to ripping out a rookie for showing up in torn shorts - "You're a bloody professional, Katu. Dress like it."- and he sank down onto the bench to yank on his cleats. Being a team player came easy to him. He liked the push and pull of theory and action, leadership and loose play. He might not be happy to be an Auckland Knight, but he had no worries about how he'd slot in to the team dynamics.

That lasted until he ran out onto the field.

The team was a fucking mess. Dropped passes, missed tackles, the defensive line speed of a lame tortoise. Harro snapped drill instructions at them in staccato bursts, his experience and frustration leaking out through the tight clench of his jaw, but the field action remained as sloppy as custard.

Manu stood on the outskirts of the team circle when they finally finished up, the familiar prickle of sweat on his skin as he squirted water into his mouth and listened half-heartedly to their captain, Matt Hollis, declaring them all a bunch of pussies and comparing their energy levels to that of his dead grandmother.

May she rest in peace.

Unlikely though, if she was Hollis's nana. The team captain was a twatwaffle of the highest order, and that kind of attitude had to come from somewhere. Hollis's late granny was likely warming her toes by the sulphur pits of the underworld.

"Ready for the showers?" Chalmers popped up in his face, drawing Manu out of his post-practice fog.

"Hmmm?" Manu shook off the daze and the flash of fear that came with it. He shouldn't feel the vestiges of fatigue dragging through him at twenty-six. He had maybe six good years left in the game if he was lucky, and if his knee held out and the concussions were minimal. Pacific Islanders didn't often last longer than the age of thirty in league. They peaked early, the explosive and energetic nature of the game designed for their youth. White boys could last longer - a slower build, consistency throughout the years - but for Island boys the window was short and sharp. Having already missed three potential earning years recovering from being hit by a car at nineteen, he couldn't afford to slow down now. Not physically. Not mentally. Resolve straightened his spine. If he only had a few seasons left in the game, he wanted to spend them winning.

"You go ahead," he told Chalmers. "I'm going to talk to Coach."

The fullback shrugged and jogged towards the stands, following the trail of players that dotted the grass between Manu and the stadium like black-and-scarlet ants.

"Coach?"

Harro grunted, his jaw working in tight movements as he stared towards the empty bleachers.

"I'd like to talk to you about my contract."

Harro barked out a laugh. "You want more money, Esera? You haven't even shown me you're worth what we paid for you yet."

"It's not about the money." Manu lifted his chin. "It's about the team."

"You gonna save us? Get us a trophy?"

"No."

Finally Harro swung his gaze towards Manu, one grizzled eyebrow raised. "No? You don't think we can make it?"

"No, I don't. Not this year. Maybe not even next. It's been over ten years since the Knights even made the top eight. One man can't make that kind of difference, and even if he could, it's a collective effort."

Harro acknowledged his words with a head tilt. "What about the team then, Esera?"

Manu drew a deep breath. "I want out." Harro just stared at him, so he carried on, nerves flickering under his skin like lightning.

"The team's crap, Coach. You picked me up cos I was going cheap after the Giants dropped me mid-season, but we both know I'm not enough to turn the season around for you. It's your first season coaching here and you've had unfortunate injuries, but the main problem is poor defence and a lack of heart. I want to make a deal."

Both of Harro's eyebrows were now hovering where his hairline used to be.

"A deal? You've just come in, insulted my players, my game plan, and you want to make a deal?"

"Yes."

"Jesus Christ." Harro shook his head. "The balls on you. Alright, Esera, what's the deal?"

"I can get you to the quarter-finals." Manu waited for a reaction but none was forthcoming. Steeling himself, he continued. "If my contribution to the team for the rest of the season means we're in the top eight at the end of pool play, I want to be traded to another top-eight team for next year. The media will be favourable to you - you're a legend, you're new to coaching in Auckland and you'll have managed to finish with the team higher on the board than anyone else in a decade. You'll have another season or two to get to the grand final. But I want to win it. And I can't do that here."

"You know I don't buy and sell the contracts, Esera. That's not how rugby league works."

"But you have a say."

Harro narrowed his eyes at Manu. "I have a say." He paused, teeth worrying his bottom lip.

"Alright then. If your performances are significant in us getting to the quarter-finals, I'll recommend we trade you to a top-eight club at the end of the season."

Relief poured over Manu like a wave. He reached out and clasped the older man's hand, shaking it firmly.

"I won't let you down."

"You better not. Bugger off and have a shower. For now you're a Knight."

A grin split Manu's face, and he let it, hope pouring out of the crack like sunlight. Turning on his heel, he headed back across the field, tugging off his Knights' training top as he did so.

Not for long.

THREE

Clare let herself into the apartment, weariness tugging at her bones as she peeled off her red coat and hung it on its hook alongside the others.

So much for red being the colour of power. The optimism she'd felt choosing her coat this morning had been swiftly punctured by her meeting with Trish. Dragging herself down the hallway, she stopped dead at the sight of Manu stretched out on the couch in a sleeveless tee and shorts, one arm flung over his eyes and an icepack on his knee. His skin was the colour of bronze and a traditional Pacific tattoo snaked up the length of his left arm and over the sliver of his chest that peeked out from behind the fabric of his top.

She smothered the unbidden groan that rose in her throat, but he shifted, moving his arm and pinning her with his dark gaze.

"Hey. How was your day?"

Chatty. Wonderful.

"Not ideal." She threw herself onto the far end of the sectional, trying very hard not to notice the muscular length of his leg, dusted with dark hair, directed towards her as she burrowed into a pile of navy velvet throw pillows.

"No fun in the science world today, huh?"

"The science is fine. The people are not."

"Ah." Manu propped his head up on a throw pillow of his own, his braided hair spilling over it like a Disney princess. "What happened?"

Out of habit, she threw him a quick glare - nothing hard, just Death Glare Number One - but he simply grinned at her.

Christ, he's good-looking. Desire hit her like a brick, weighty and sharp-edged, sitting uncomfortably in her chest. Their increased interactions were doing nothing to diminish his beauty. In fact, seeing him like this was worse. The smooth bunch of his bicep as he tucked one arm under his head, the slippery fabric of his clothes ghosting over the hard lines of his chest, stomach and thighs, leaving *nothing* to the imagination - her resistance was wilting under the reckless enthusiasm of her horniness, which leapt forth like an eager puppy.

Her gaze ate him up, travelling hungrily over his body - firm where she was soft, dark where she was pale - until she reached his face.

Any sense of friendliness had fled. His brown eyes were hot, intensity etched in the lines around his eyes, the clench of his jaw. The tension swirled between them, thick and red, almost malicious in the way it picked apart her defences, leaving her breathlessly locked in Manu's charged gaze.

Then he moved. Raising himself up to a sitting position, he looked for all the world like he was about to drag her into his lap and devour her.

Thud!

The icepack bounced off the hardwood, clattering to a stop by her foot and smacking her back into reality.

"People hate me." The words were out before she could stop them, a desperate yelp that punctured the air, releasing the heat that shimmered in front of her vision as she ripped her gaze from his.

She heard a noise - a loaded exhale.

"I'm sure that's not true," he responded, and she thanked Marie Curie for him picking up the ruined threads of their conversation and stitching it back together.

"It is." She nodded vigorously, keeping her eyes on the floor. "My boss told me today. Apparently it's not enough for me to be able to create life in a petri dish. I need to be able to smile more when it's happening."

"That's what you do?"

She shrugged one shoulder casually, as if she hadn't fought tooth and nail for every grade, lab result and opportunity that had gotten her to where she was.

"I'm a team leader at North Hope Fertility Centre. There are four teams in total, made up of embryologists, andrology scientists and nurses. We share doctors who rotate. It's a bigger operation than most other clinics and they found it easier to divide us that way. Our lab manager, Trish, is leaving soon. I want her job and applications open in six weeks, but she told me today that my client feedback blows. I'm not friendly enough, they don't think I care about their feelings. I'm trying my best to give them a baby for God's sake. What more do they want?"

"That sucks."

She glanced over at him, wary of the jet stream of heat she'd left behind, but he was watching her benignly.

"Yeah," she exhaled. "It does."

"So what are you going to do about it?"

Confusion pulled at her brow. "What do you mean?"

Manu shrugged, the smooth camber of his shoulders rising and falling hypnotically. "You have an obstacle. You have six weeks to find a way around it. What do you need to do to win?"

"This isn't a game."

"Isn't it? Are there any other team leaders who want the job?"

Clare faltered, the memory of James hovering outside her performance review dancing in her memory.

"Yes..." She drew the word out haltingly. "I'm sure there are."

"So that's your opposition. Trish is your referee. You've got to find a way to show her you're the champion. Who's on your team?"

"My actual team? Like the one I lead?"

"Your metaphorical team."

"Oh. Nobody."

"What?"

Clare risked another look at Manu. The confusion on his face tempered some of the absurd attractiveness.

"Nobody's on my team," she repeated.

"Oh." Confusion gave way to understanding and he nodded. "You're a show pony."

"A what?"

"A show pony. You keep the glory for yourself. Don't pass the ball, don't share the limelight, that kind of thing."

Clare balked, righteous indignation swelling inside her. "People want the best in my line of work. I am the best. That's just a fact. I don't need to rely on other people to do my job."

His honeyed chuckle slid through her, and she did her best not to squirm. "Sure, baby. But nobody's the best by themselves. Trust me, I've been playing games my whole adult life, on the field and off. The only way you can make any progress is if there are people that have your back, people you can rely on when the going gets tough. Every franchise has a captain, but leaders need others to follow them. Into battle, onto the field, towards goals. If you want this promotion, you're going to need a team."

Clare mulled his words over. Tex would be on her team if he was in town. *Stupid Tex, leaving me here with this guy instead.* The thought struck her out of nowhere. "Will you be on my team?" As soon as she voiced the idea, it clicked into place inside her with the iridescent buzz that came when she was truly onto something in the lab.

Manu recoiled slightly, the intensity in his eyes wavering as a flash of something -*doubt?* - flickered in their depths. "I don't know anything about science."

She snorted. "I don't need help with science. I need help with people. You seem nice enough, you have the confidence to approach strangers in the pub, you look like *that"* - she waved a hand in his general direction - "and apparently you're a team player. You must know how to make people like you. I was going to look for a YouTube tutorial, but this is much better."

He looked a little dazed. "You were going to learn how to make people like you off YouTube?"

"Sure. That's how I learnt to make Pad Thai."

"Those ... are not the same things."

Clare rolled her eyes, huffing out an impatient breath. "Whatever. Will you help me or not?"

"Is that how your mother taught you to ask for a favour?" His voice was light now, teasing her.

"I don't have a mother," she responded flatly. Saying it didn't slice her open in thin ribbons anymore, but the thick pinch of rejection still twanged low in her gut. When he didn't respond, she rolled her eyes and tried again. "Please, Manu, will you teach me how to make people like me in the next six weeks so I can get my promotion?"

He was quiet for a moment, and she thought she'd blown it, until ... "I don't have a mother either. Alright, Clare." His warm amusement hadn't gone anywhere, but the low gravel tone sent goosebumps skittering over her skin. "I'll be your social Yoda. Help you I will."

———

MANU STARED after Clare in bemused wonder as she pranced into the kitchen to make herself a celebratory coffee. She was a bona fide weirdo, and he was into it. God help him when she actually started putting in effort. Effort *he* was supposed to facilitate. What had he gotten himself into?

Quickly he categorised the strengths and weaknesses he'd seen in their short acquaintance. The eye-rolling would have to go first. It was a miracle she hadn't sprained an optic nerve by now. She was blunt and prickly and used 'please' and 'thank you' with the consistency of a kindergartener.

Unbidden, the image of Clare tied to the generic, sexless headboard in his room, gasping the word 'please', floated to the forefront of his brain, almost knocking the breath from him with a throat-punch of desire. The effect was instantaneous, blazing down his spine to pull taut between his legs. This was a bad idea, he could feel it in his bones and in the heated stream of his blood, but for some reason the thought of falling into Clare didn't fill him with the tingling sense of dread he usually associated with relationships.

He closed his eyes and concentrated on his most passion-dulling memory, pulling the details out of the drawer in his mind he kept them locked in and examining them one by one. The warm concrete beneath him, the hollow shouts in his native Avalian language. The hot scream of pain in his right knee, the thick bite of nausea in his windpipe, his best friend, Tua's, lifeless body beside him, and the hard snaps of camera shutters flickering without pause or empathy, taking in every grimy detail of his suffering.

He waited, holding the images in his mind until the roar of passion in his ears faded and he could breathe easily again. If ever there was a reminder of how blindly following temptation led to disaster, it was the accident. Maybe it hadn't been *his* temptation, but it had been his disaster nonetheless.

Clare sauntered back into the room and dropped onto the far end of the couch. Black coffee sloshed over the side of her mug, running in tiny rivulets that left streaks on the white ceramic.

"Bugger." She rubbed at the folds of her black blouse, trying to disguise the spots that had landed on it rather than remove them. "Okay then, Obi-Wan. Dazzle me." She licked a trail up the side of her mug, trying to catch any stray droplets, and the telltale rush sounded in his ears again.

"The pub," he blurted, suddenly desperate for noise and distraction and public eyes, which would surely dissuade him from palming his cock to the thought of his off-limits flatmate.

"What?" Her grey gaze blinked at him over the rim of her mug.

"Let's go to the pub." His voice was slightly higher than normal, but maybe she wouldn't notice.

"We can't go to the pub tonight." Clare was looking at him like he was an idiot.

Better an idiot than a pervert.

"Why not?"

"It's Wednesday."

Manu waited, tension still strumming through him, but she didn't seem inclined to offer any further explanation.

"You don't go to the pub on Wednesdays?"

"It's quiz night," the object of his lust explained with a long-suffering sigh, as though explaining the schedule to a small child and not somebody who'd lived in the building for less than twenty-four hours.

Manu shrugged. "I don't see the problem," he said. "Why can't you go to the pub on quiz night? You should put a team together. You're smart. You'd probably destroy the rest of them."

"I'm only smart about certain things," Clare mumbled, her eyes downcast. "And it's full of strangers. Strangers make me uncomfortable."

A full-bodied chuckle rumbled out of his chest. He had her now, and the relief of being only moments from the bustle of the pub made him almost giddy. "Well, you're going to have to get used to them if you want your promotion, Clare. Pour that into a travel cup. It's not like you have to talk to them. But being in a social setting is important - you need to be comfortable making conversation in a neutral environment. We'll have a bit of a chat and use your enormous brain to win the bar tab, and then you can carry on being an antisocial loner tomorrow."

"I wish you were more antisocial," she grumbled under

her breath as she hauled herself off the couch and moved towards the kitchen.

"No you don't," he called after her cheerfully, heading to his room to change. "But I'll make you a deal. If we place in the top three in the quiz tonight, I won't make you go back again next week."

When he'd finished pulling on sweatpants, shoes and a lightweight Knights jacket, he ventured out into the hallway to find Clare standing in front of her rainbow rack of coats and glaring at the red one.

"Has your coat offended you in some way?"

"Broken promises," she muttered darkly, grabbing the blue one down. "Here." She thrust a daisy-printed travel cup into his hands, and he cradled the warm mug in his hands while she drew on her blue coat. He tried hard not to notice the swish of her dark hair or the scent of lemons mingled with black coffee that teased his nostrils.

The gangly blond from the night before did a double take when they walked in. He opened his mouth, but Clare stopped him with a raised palm.

"I don't want to hear it, Cole."

"You're probably going to though." The bartender looked between her and Manu. "This is your doing?"

"I suggested we come here tonight." Obviously something was at play he wasn't privy to, but he didn't much care now that the presence of witnesses had significantly decreased the likelihood of him trying to stick his tongue down his flatmate's throat.

The woman in question snorted when the other man began a slow clap. "So dramatic. What time does the quiz start?"

"Forty minutes. Grab a table. I think the back booth is free. Are you eating?"

"I'll have the usual." Clare looked towards Manu. "Have you had dinner?"

He shook his head and quickly perused the stack of menus by the register. "I'll have the lamb salad please."

"Anything to drink?"

"Just water."

Both Clare and Cole looked at him strangely, but he was used to that when he ordered food during training. With his deal with Harro secured, he wasn't risking his career on a basket of chicken wings.

Cole placed a lurid pink soda on the bar in front of Clare and she picked it up with the hand that wasn't holding her coffee.

God, she looks like a walking advertisement for hypertension.

She just blinked at him, seemingly oblivious to his concern for her arteries. "Let's get this over with then."

He followed obediently, keeping his eyes very firmly on the back of her head and not the tempting sway of her hips. He waited while she placed both drinks on the table of the booth where they'd met last night and shrugged out of her coat. She threw it into the booth and followed it in, arranging her drinks precisely equal distance from her once seated.

So weird. I like it.

He plopped down in the seat opposite her. "Okay. Let's start at the very beginning."

She shot him a dirty look. "Is that a reference to *The Sound of Music*?"

"It is. Think of yourself as Liesel. You're suspicious of strangers and you have terrible taste in men."

"What makes you think I have terrible taste in men?"

"You shot me down when I made a move last night. I am

awesome. Therefore, you must be attracted to men who are not awesome."

Clare sputtered like an angry goldfish on dry land.

"Or women," Manu supplied helpfully. "You may also have terrible taste in women."

He was saved by Cole slapping a thin quiz booklet and a pen down on the polished wood between them, followed by a frosted bottle of water with a gentler hand.

"Meals will be up in ten." He glanced between them. "You guys alright?"

Manu leaned back in the booth and grinned at Clare. She looked like she wanted to maim him. It was precious.

"We're fine," his companion ground out, glaring daggers at him.

Cole sighed. "Just try not to get blood on the upholstery." He retreated back towards the bar.

Smart guy.

Clare opened her mouth but Manu got there first.

"I'm just teasing. But we can use last night as a starting point. I was a stranger trying to make casual conversation with you. The reaction I got was not positive. I can appreciate that, in the sense of me being a man and approaching you, who I'm assuming identifies as a woman, in a drinking establishment and all of the cultural meaning that is attached to such an interaction. You told me to fuck off, and off I fucked. But with work, you're going to want to present a more welcoming tone. Let's practice."

He stood up and walked around the small space at the back of the bar, ignoring the other patrons who had been steadily filing in since they'd sat down. Straightening his spine, he puffed out his chest a little, pasted on the smile that had caused one sports blogger to dub him 'The Panty-Melter of Polynesia' and headed back towards the booth.

Pick Up Attempt 2.0.

FOUR

He slid into the booth, more aware this time of the shine of the bar lights on her black hair, the wariness in her grey eyes, and the impenetrable aura of 'Leave me alone' radiating from her like a human Chernobyl.

"Hi, I'm Manu." He waited.

"I'm Clare."

Her voice was hesitant, still chilly, but he wasn't sure if that was due to the roleplay or her general reaction towards him.

"May I sit here?

The eye roll was back, but a small smile tugged at the corners of her mouth. "You may."

"Thank you." He leaned back, stretching his arms along the wooden railing and reducing the intimacy the small booth created.

"How long do you normally spend with each client?"

Clare drained her coffee cup and reached for the pink monstrosity.

"They're called patients. And about fifteen minutes usually. Doctors and nurses do most of the face to face because they administer the tests, collect the samples and deliver the results. I'm really just there to stick a baby in them and go."

"So small talk is going to be the best tool in your offence. These people are nervous, you're holding their dreams in your hand and you're gone in an instant. You need them to remember you as kind, funny and supportive."

Clare just stared at him, her nose slightly wrinkled. "Uh-huh." She didn't sound convinced.

Manu grinned, the rush of excitement that always came before a game leaking into his veins. He wouldn't stop it if he could. The thrill of a challenge was music to his ears, food to his soul, the very fabric of his being, and Clare - *Clare's promotion* - gave him the opportunity to win something, albeit indirectly. Hell, he was more likely to see success helping her with her job situation than playing in the next six weeks of round-robin play with the Knights.

"Come on then," he encouraged her, as Cole placed a lamb salad in front of him and the world's largest plate of steak and chips in front of her. "Small talk can be anything. Ask me my favourite dinosaur or my shoe size."

"I don't care about your shoe size."

"Is that being kind, funny and supportive?"

Clare ignored the snort that came from the retreating bartender, picking up a chip and nibbling on the end as she eyed him.

"Alright," she said suddenly. "What's your middle name?"

"Mikaele," Manu replied promptly. "It's the Avalian version of Michael. Michael means 'God-like', you know. What's yours?"

"Never mind." She bit into another chip and fired

another question at him around a mouthful of potato. "How old are you?"

"Twenty-six."

"I'm twenty-eight."

"You look younger."

"It's the peace that comes from living in solitude."

"When do you turn twenty-nine?"

"May sixth."

"Ah, a Taurus." He nodded sagely, picking up his fork. "It all makes sense now."

Clare groaned, cutting her steak with surgical precision. "You believe in astrology?"

Manu waited until he'd had a chance to properly appreciate his first forkful of tender lamb before answering. "The stars are an important part of my culture in every way. Avalian people believe that birth dates and times have meaning, yes."

"What's your star sign then?"

"Pisces."

"And would you consider yourself a typical Piscean?"

"More or less." He shrugged.

"Hmm." She eyed him over the rim of her glass. "Favourite food?"

"Chocolate cheesecake."

"Place you'd most like to visit?"

"Antarctica."

They ran through the list of his basic stats for the rest of the meal, stuff anyone could find on his Wikipedia page. Manu relaxed into their conversation, leaning forward in the booth to hear over the growing crowd as Clare fired questions at him like an inquisitor.

"Film character you would swap places with?"

"Han Solo."

"Typical. Any siblings?"

The warning ran through him like an electric current, leaving goosebumps in its wake.

"One brother," he answered slowly, his mind racing to search for an out.

"Older or younger?"

"Older."

"What does he do?"

Bugger.

"He's a prince."

"A what?" Clare thunked her soda down.

"A prince. He, um, he's the heir to the throne of Avali."

"Right." Clare's tone was incredulous, but he kept his gaze glued to a leftover smear of yogurt-mint dressing on his plate. "And what are you then?"

"Also a prince."

Long beats of silence lumbered through the air between them, thick and heavy. He twisted his fingers together under the table, rubbing his right thumb across the solid band of silver engraved with the Avalian crest that he wore on his left. When Clare spoke again, her words echoed airily above him, as though the distance that existed between them on every level now extended to her voice.

"You expect me to believe that the guy sleeping in my spare bedroom is a prince of one of the Pacific Island's most progressive nations?"

Manu sighed and flipped his wallet out of his jacket pocket and onto the table. Turquoise nails flashed in his peripherals as she flipped it open to reveal his Avalian driver's licence.

His Royal Highness Manu Mikaele Esera.

He knew the words by heart, he'd seen and heard them

a thousand times, but Clare ran her thumb across them as if discovering a new language.

"What the *fuck*—"

He flinched at her tone, knowing what was coming.

"—are you doing playing bloody sports for a living?"

There it is.

No matter how hard he tried to avoid it, the same question came up every time. Frustration blazed through him and he gritted his teeth against the impulse to raise his voice.

"I'm not good at politics."

Her laugh was almost unhinged. "Not *good* at it? What does that mean?"

"I'm not a good leader." He raised his eyes to hers, the blade of his irritation softening at the confusion written across her gorgeous face. "Geography, systems of government, policies. None of it makes sense to me."

"But surely there are people to help you with all that? And you could learn a lot of it too. Did you study political science at university?"

"I didn't go to university." She gaped at him, but it was too late to turn back now. "I didn't even finish high school."

"But ... your parents."

He laughed, bitterness flooding the back of his throat. "My mother died when I was a year old. My father didn't take it well. He's not a bad man, but he was never particularly interested in Aleki or I. Aleki gets more of his attention, being the heir to the throne and now engaged with a baby on the way, but I'm just the spare. And nobody cares how the spare spends his days."

"I'm sure that's not true."

"Sure it is. Look at Harry. Told them all to go fuck themselves. Just off in America, living his best life with his incredible wife. He's as inspirational to second-born royals as he is to gingers."

Clare's brow furrowed. "Were there no teachers who could help you?"

"It's not that I can't pass high school, Clare. I just didn't. I got scouted as an upcoming talent in league when I was fourteen. Do you know how hard it is to get noticed when you're playing against kids three years older than you on grounds as hard as cement? I knew right then, as soon as I was approached, that this career is what I wanted. I skipped school, put in extra hours at practice or the gym, worked my arse off for my first contract. I'm still working my arse off for contracts. And, for the most part, that contract money goes towards education services and medical equipment and anything else that Avali needs to provide the best life possible for our people on the island. That's what I do. That's how I serve my people."

Conviction and shame ran a dual line through his veins as he finished speaking. Logically he knew he was right, but the distress in Clare's eyes amplified the insecurity that always pulsed deep down in his chest. Maybe he wasn't good enough. Maybe he never would have made it at school, even if he'd tried.

Enough. He pushed the thought away. He'd done what he needed to in order to get where he wanted to be.

Forcing a grin on his face, he grabbed the quiz booklet and scrawled a team name in the space provided.

Team Seki.

Team Awesome.

"Enough about me. Come on, Booksmart. Let's see how you go without me in the sports round."

CLARE STARED UNSEEING down the length of the conference table, breathing through the roil of acid in her chest. It had taken up residence approximately thirteen hours ago when Manu had shown her his driver's licence and had remained an acid yellow band since. From the quiz, where Manu's quiet, tight-lipped answers had secured them third place, through to this morning, when there had been nothing but empty silence in the apartment as she showered and got ready for work.

"Good morning, Clare. Did you do anything fun last night?"

"Hmmm?" She jerked her attention towards the voice. Jeremy, obviously. She turned her attention back to the table. "Went to a pub quiz. What about you? I assume you felled half a forest and then built a log cabin with your bare hands."

"Naturally. Then my boyfriend and I roasted marsh-mallows on the open fire and shagged on the bear skin rug. It was brilliant."

"Do people still have bear skin rugs?"

"I wouldn't know. Ethan only books us into environ-mentally friendly eco-lodges when we go on holiday. The last one made us take wheatgrass shots each morning. It was awful." He paused. "Great linens though."

Clare looked back towards him, suspicion crawling over her.

I didn't know he was in a relationship. What else don't I know?

"Jeremy?"

"Clare?"

"Are you applying for Trish's job when she leaves at the end of the year?"

"No."

The suspicion slid away, satisfaction settling into its place.

"James is though."

Fuck.

"How do you know that?"

"He warned me off it when I first started here." Jeremy paused again. "Bit of a knobhead, that one."

"Hmmm," she replied noncommittally.

Accurate.

"Do you want to have lunch today?"

"No." The word flew out automatically, hanging in the air between them like a large black balloon.

"Okay."

"I eat lunch at my desk."

"Every day?"

"Yes."

Jeremy turned away, his gaze fixed down the long table and the knot in Clare's stomach pulled tighter.

First Manu, now Jeremy. Why couldn't she ever be nice to people who were trying to help her?

She twisted her fingers under the table as Trish barked out instructions and relevant information for the day ahead, and her mind wandered back to the disastrous quiz night. She wasn't naturally inclined to notice when others weren't happy, with the obvious exception of Tex, who'd first punched a wall in front of her at the tender age of twelve. Manu, though, had been such an irrepressible ray of sunshine so far that his downcast eyes and clipped, one-word answers had seemed the equivalent of him openly carving plans to murder her in the polished wooden table.

Definitely not happy with me.

In retrospect, she could see why. Career choices were

like family - at least she assumed they were - in that you could criticise your own but not other people's.

But, honestly, what is he thinking?

Who in their right mind turned their back on being royalty to roll around in the mud with multiple other men fighting over a ball?

Mind you, he had mentioned something about his money going back to help his country, although at the time it had barely registered through the rushing in her ears.

Stealthily, she slid her phone from her scrubs pocket and opened her search engine. Typing in 'Manu Esera' brought up a slew of pages. His official stuff with the Knights and, before them, the Giants, and a clutch of *excellent* photos, including some of him naked holding a strategically placed ball and a select few of him in official Avalian dress participating in various events.

He was rarely the focus of the Avalian shots, usually standing several feet behind two other men - one older, stooped but solid, and one who looked like a before picture of Manu, slimmer and shinier, with short glossy hair. But Manu was there, opening libraries, attending concerts and even greeting foreign dignitaries, wearing formal button downs, lavalavas and leis.

The sight of him in something other than casual training gear sent a shiver of awareness through her.

Holy hotness, Batman.

A sharp poke to her thigh distracted her from the hum building between her legs, and she jerked her head up.

Trish was staring at her expectantly.

"Sorry, could you repeat the question?" Under the table Jeremy slipped her phone from her hands, but Clare could hardly wrestle it back under their boss's watchful gaze.

Trish pursed her lips and exhaled through her nose. "I was wondering if you wanted to give us an overview of the new nursing roster you're trialling in your team."

"Oh, um, yep." Clare looked back across the table. Hilary was watching her sympathetically and James wasn't even bothering to hide a self-satisfied smirk.

"Some of the nurses on my team were finding it difficult with the current roster, so we're trialling a system now that uses the four-day work week model with an opt-in system for on-call. The justification is that it gives staff who are parents a better idea on a long-term basis of how to arrange childcare, and those who are looking for extra hours can work them into a schedule that they're comfortable with. Obviously we'll need to see how this progresses through periods like the Christmas holidays, but we start next week and buy-in from the team has been high."

In fact, she'd overheard nurses from the other teams complaining about not being able to participate in the trial run.

"Curious to see how that goes. Can't imagine all those mums lining up to opt in for call shifts." James spoke lightly, tapping his fingers on the table, and Clare risked Death Glare Number One at him.

"Not all of the parents on our nursing staff are female, James." Trish's voice could cut diamonds. "Good initiative, Clare," she offered in a softer tone, and Clare just about fell off her chair in relief. "Keep me updated."

Clare nodded frantically as Trish dismissed them, then flopped back in her seat while the others filed out.

Most of the others.

Jeremy was still in the seat next to her. He had her phone out above the table now, scrolling through it.

"Did not pick you for the big and burly type." He glinted a wicked smile at her. "Secret jock fantasies from high school, Miss Trescott?"

Clare snatched her phone back, shutting down the window Jeremy had open - Manu, under a waterfall, wearing only chest hair and a smile, the pool of water *just* covering his groin. *How on Earth does that promote sports?*

"He's my flatmate," she muttered.

Jeremy quirked a brow. "Interesting. Maybe I'll join you for lunch at your desk today. You can tell me all about what he looks like when he gets out of the shower."

"What about Ethan?"

"We'll call him on speaker phone. He can listen too."

Amusement licked at Clare and a reluctant smile tugged at her lips.

"Besides," Jeremy continued, "Esera's a quality league player, royalty, and looking at his face too long is like staring into the sun. Ethan will be lucky if I don't immediately move into your place and enjoy the view in person."

"You know he's a prince?" Shock echoed in her words.

"Clare." Jeremy's gaze was chock-full of pity. "*Everyone* knows he's a prince."

She winced. Obviously her current affairs knowledge was as up-to-date as her sports trivia.

Just then her phone beeped. She swiped the message open.

Unknown number: *It's Manu. Think we need another run at your small talk game. No quiz this time. I'm playing on Saturday evening, so how does tomorrow night sound for dinner? My treat.*

It felt like a royal pardon. Relief flooded her system. At least now she could go home before midnight instead of avoiding him. She typed out a quick reply.

Okay.

Jeremy, reading over her shoulder, snorted.

"Oh, God. You're in so much trouble."

FIVE

Recapping the bottle of hot pink nail polish, Clare checked the face of the watch Tex had gifted her with when she graduated from uni.

Seven minutes to go.

A hoard of hummingbirds flitted through her intestines, their tiny wings thrumming wildly and beating up a sea of tension that spread through her, from the freshly painted tips of her fingers to her toes, safe and warm in her leopard print ankle boots.

It's just pretend. It doesn't mean anything.

Her firm mental reminder did nothing to quell the storm of nerves inside her.

She hadn't seen Manu since his text the day before, as she'd stayed at work until after nine prepping samples for pre-implantation genetic diagnosis and updating patient files. When she'd snuck in, his door had been shut and only a single light was left on in the kitchen. He'd been gone this morning, the steamed up mirror in the bathroom the only sign he'd even been there.

She smoothed her simple black knee-length dress down

over the curve of her stomach and checked her appearance in the mirror. Hair straightened and down around her shoulders, a heavy hand with the mascara and a swipe of pink lip colour. She'd put in more effort for this fake pity/training date than she had the last time she'd attempted a romantic entanglement.

Oliver. The dentist. Terrible table manners. Mediocre sex.

She'd been up and out of his Parnell townhouse before the wet spot had dried.

A frisson ran through her at the thought of sex with Manu. Of seeing his huge body in all its glory, acres of brown skin and ink stretched over slabs of muscle, his full lips on hers, big hands exploring her body, the power and heat and athleticism of him all focused on her, her pleasure, on making her feel good.

Clare's nipples tightened under the fabric of her dress as she imagined the scrape of his teeth across her neck, the bite of his short nails in the flesh of her hips as he dragged her close.

"Clare?"

The object of her fantasy stood in her doorway in a black suit and white shirt with the collar unbuttoned, hair slicked back in a low bun, looking like the ultimate prize in the straight women's sexual lottery.

Oh yeah, Manu Esera would be *great* in bed.

"Ready to go?"

"Definitely." Clare snatched her purse up off the bed and slung its thin silver chain over her shoulder. Their date might be fake, but her attraction to Manu was real as hell and Clare had always been a big fan of following through on attraction. Men like Oliver the Dentist were fine as placeholders during a dry spell, but someone like Manu was likely to make her vagina sing the Hallelujah chorus. And it was a very long time since she'd seen the light.

Seemingly unaware of her lusty thoughts, Manu followed her down the hallway to collect her black wool coat - it was winter after all - and then out and into the lift. Once on the street, he ushered her into the waiting Uber and stayed blessedly silent on the way to the restaurant while Clare compiled a mental pros-cons list about boning her new flatmate.

Pros: His lease is only for eight weeks. Eight weeks of in-house orgasms is nothing to sneeze at.

Cons: He won't leave the premises when we finish.

Rebuttal Pros: Could result in further orgasms.

Rebuttal Cons: None. Go for it.

That was that then. Determination straightened her spine and she reached across the small sedan's seat to place her hand on Manu's thigh.

Holy hell, it's like concrete.

"Thanks for helping me, Manu. I appreciate it."

He was watching her warily. She gave him her most dazzling smile, the one she'd practiced in the mirror for hours before meeting potential foster families, and a crinkle formed between his brows.

"Right." He drew the word out, the lilt of his accent rolling the 'R' around in his mouth like an expensive wine.

She hoped he could do more with that mouth.

The car pulled to a stop and she hopped out and rounded the car towards where he stood on the sidewalk, confidence in her veins. She didn't like people, and they didn't like her, but she *did* like sex and had never had any trouble attracting it. Sure, she never usually spoke to her sexual partners again after their encounters, let alone shared a bathroom with one, but with their work schedules she was unlikely to see him much outside of night hours.

Her confidence lasted until their starters arrived.

"Why are you being weird?" He dropped the question into their discussion around the benefits of yoga as he leaned over to snag a prawn off her plate.

"What do you mean?" Her response was abstracted, most of her attention focused on trying to stab his thieving hand with her entree fork.

"You're acting like you've been told I'm dying."

"I'm trying to be nice."

"It's creepy. Stop it."

"Fine." Sullenness crept into her voice and she slumped in her chair. "I thought that was kind of the point of this though."

"You're supposed to be practicing small talk, not looking at me like you're assessing me for human trafficking potential. You look at your patients like that and you're gonna be on sperm-sample duty before you can blink."

She sniffed. "The nurses do that. And I wasn't assessing you for your human trafficking potential. I was assessing you for your sexual-satisfaction potential."

The clang of his fork as it fell to his plate echoed throughout the restaurant. The hushed conversations of their fellow diners paused as they craned their heads towards their table, and a well-dressed waiter started towards them. Manu waved him off. He waited until the low hum of noise picked up again before leaning forward over the table.

"What do you mean by that?" His voice was pitched low, his eyes were hot, and Clare was suddenly keenly, achingly aware of the throb between her legs.

She sighed loudly. "Don't be dramatic, Manu. You're a good-looking guy. It's natural that I'd wonder."

"Wonder what?"

"What you're like in bed." She shrugged and lifted her glass of water to her lips. "It's nothing personal."

He made a choking sound. "You're wondering what I'm like in bed, but it's *nothing personal*?" Incredulity raised his voice towards the end of his sentence and Clare smirked.

Gotcha.

"Sure. It's just curiosity. Don't you wonder about me?"

Fascination reverberated through her as she watched him grit his teeth.

"Yes."

"Well then," she replied briskly. "There you go. Perfectly natural. Are you going to finish that paua ravioli?"

He stared at her in wonder. "You are the devil."

She raised her eyebrows at him. "Now who needs to learn how to be nicer?"

That was pretty much it for the rest of the meal. Manu stared moodily at his water glass through the mains, and Clare took full advantage of not having to practice her bedside manner by scarfing down her venison carpaccio in blessed silence.

Manu maintained his brooding all through the ride home. When they were finally walking back through the brightly lit lobby of Tex's apartment building, she leaned over and patted his arm.

"Thanks for our fake date."

He grunted, audibly grinding his teeth. That couldn't be good for his enamel. Maybe she should give him Oliver's number and he could schedule a check-up.

The lift arrived and he followed her in. Their gazes

clashed in the mirror at the back of the carriage as the doors closed behind them.

He was on her in an instant, spinning her and pressing her against the cool glass, his mouth hot and sweet. She drank him in, the lingering taste of burnt butter sauce, the firm press of his tongue, and her hands glided up to burrow in the silky hair at his temples. He groaned into her mouth, ragged and raw, and she sank her teeth into his bottom lip and tugged, satisfaction and pleasure weaving a heady smugness through her at the evidence of his desire pressing against her pelvis.

He pulled back and stared at her, and anticipation licked through her at the hunger in his dark eyes.

"Does that feel fake to you?"

"No," she gasped, pressing her hips forward against his very, very real erection and letting her head fall back against the mirror as black spots danced in front of her eyes.

The ding of the lift cleared her head a little, and then he was dragging her out of the steel box, down the hallway and fumbling with the keys outside the door of 5A, while she unbuttoned her coat as fast as she could manage with fingers that were suddenly too big and clumsy.

Then they were inside, the hallway wall at her back, the heat of him at her front, and in the distance she heard the clatter of keys falling to the wooden floor as he slid calloused palms up the smooth expanse of her bare thighs - *Thank Marie Curie I didn't wear tights* - and lifted. She wrapped her legs around his thick hips, burrowing her boots into the small of his back and nestling him tighter into the vee of her legs. He rasped out a curse and tugged the modest neckline of her dress down, licking and sucking and biting her exposed throat and collarbone. The abrasive sensation of stubble sent white-capped waves of lust shooting through her as she ground her pelvis against him.

So good, so good, so good.

Teeth nipped at her earlobe and she almost squirmed out of his hands, but he gripped the cheeks of her arse tighter and yanked her higher up his body to pin her in place while he did it again.

"Oh fuck yes, that," she whimpered, craning her neck to allow him better access, and then he hiked her again, repositioning her, and one of his hands was slipping under the soaking edge of her underwear. Relief flooded her, dizzying in its rightness as one blunt finger traced the slick seam of her body and eased into her, and she let her head fall onto Manu's shoulder as he muttered a stream of words in a language she didn't understand against her temple.

He added another finger and curved them, his thumb finding the bundle of nerves above her entrance and she gasped. Starbursts exploded behind her eyes, the tight points of her breasts rubbing against his chest as he stroked, stoking the fire higher and higher in her until she broke, grinding her forehead into the curve of his neck as she flooded his hand.

She came back to herself slowly, reality filtering through in starts - the tender kisses on her cheek, the gentle restoration of her knickers, the slow slide of her body downward until her boots hit the floor. Still, she clung to Manu, holding him tight in the darkness as the muted sound of traffic outside and the light switch digging into her scapula registered.

She exhaled heavily, a shuddering sound that would have mortified her in the light.

"Condom?"

Every muscle in Manu's body stiffened. Not just the fun one.

"Excuse me?"

"Do you have a condom?"

He moved slightly, easing away from her, though his hands still rested on her hips and her wrists were still looped around his neck. The space between them ran over her like cold water.

"No."

"No?" *Whoops, that was a bit high-pitched.* "You don't carry condoms?"

"No." His voice was firmer now, louder in the dark of the hallway.

"That seems irresponsible."

"I'm extremely responsible." An edge of something ran through his words, but she was too preoccupied to examine it.

"I might have one in my handbag."

"I'm not having sex with you, Clare."

The chill that had stolen between them grew, settling over her like a thin layer of ice, and she dropped her hands to her sides, the slide of rejection slicing through her with easy familiarity.

"Right." Her voice sounded odd to her own ears. "Fun's over then, is it?" She stepped to the side, but he clasped her wrist to prevent her moving further away.

"It's complicated."

"Oh, bugger off." She yanked her arm but it was like being held in a particularly gentle vice. "I'm not a child, Manu. I get it. I'm fun to fix but not fun enough to fuck." Mortification pricked behind her eyes, hot and scarlet.

"It's not that." He took a step forward and she immediately backed up, the initial arctic blast of dismissal giving way to the weightier prickle at the base of her skull. After eighteen years in the foster system, she recognised the feeling of being rebuffed. It clamoured at the edges of her brain, whispering its age-old taunt in a singsong voice.

Nobody wants you, nobody wants you, nobody wants you.

She wrestled it down, smothering it until she could hear the jagged edge of her breathing over the murmurs of her past.

"Of course it is. Don't worry, Manu, I'm a big girl. You can just tell me you don't want me." She hit the light switch, flooding the hall in harsh halogen beams. Might as well get this over with. He blinked at her, running one hand over his stubbled jaw.

"I *do* want you. But sex isn't on the table."

She forced out a laugh, high and false, dripping with bitterness.

"You patronising git. You're a professional athlete, but you expect me to believe you draw the line at a one-night stand?"

"Yes."

"You must be a publicist's wet dream. Prince Manu the Saint."

"I'm not a saint. I'm celibate."

"What?"

"I don't - I *haven't* - had sex since I was nineteen."

"By choice?" She sounded like a chipmunk on helium.

"Yes."

Time slowed, thick, heavy beats echoing sluggishly in her mind.

"Bullshit."

He met her eyes directly. "No."

"Let go of my arm."

He dropped her wrist instantly and she backed up the hallway. His gaze stayed locked on hers, open and trusting, a little vulnerable.

He's telling the truth.

Nausea rose in the back of her throat. She'd pursued him, she'd practically jumped him in the hallway, and here he was telling her he didn't do that sort of thing.

Panic slid up her arms. She hadn't asked if he wanted it. She *always* asked. Too many years watching others give away parts of themselves they weren't ready for had drummed that into her. *What if he didn't want to? What if he felt pressured because he lives with me or he felt sorry for me?*

The hot prick of tears pressed behind her eyes and she took in a shaky breath as the grip of anxiety long controlled by medication took hold.

Her throat constricted, and she forced the words out, taut and desperate.

"I'm sorry. I'm so sorry."

And then she fled.

MANU DRAGGED himself out of bed the next morning as frustration stretched under his skin. Last night's cold shower, combined with the horror on Clare's face when he'd told her he was celibate, had dulled all of the passion that had coursed through his body the night before, but it hadn't drained the well of tension.

That tension strummed through him as he rubbed liniment on his knee and pulled on his warm-up gear. He wasn't playing until five tonight, but the desire to get a hit out, to take the knocks and smash something into the ground, to release some of the pressure inside, was intense.

He wanted to talk to Clare to clear the air, but when he ventured into the hallway, her door was shut tight. He hovered for a moment, listening for signs of life, but heard none. If the last few days were any indication, she'd remain that way until she was sure he was gone. Clare Trescott was not one to seek out an interaction at the best of times, and these were most definitely not the best of times. Of course, there was always the possibility she was asleep.

He snuck quietly past her bedroom, the part of his mind that wasn't tangled in regret focused on getting caffeine into his system, and stopped dead when he rounded the corner to the living areas.

A hulking giant of a man stood shirtless in the apartment's small kitchen.

Horror punched through Manu, leaving nausea in its wake. Had Clare left last night, while he tortured himself in his frigid shower replaying their hallway interlude and his awkward revelation over and over in his head? Had she been so sexually frustrated that she'd gone out and found what appeared to be a leftover Hemsworth brother to entertain herself with? Manu was in the prime of his fitness, but this man looked like he bench pressed dump trucks three times a day.

Drawing himself up to his full height, Manu stepped into the tight space.

"Who the fuck are you?" His demand echoed off the gleaming white tiles.

The intruder turned slowly. Hazel eyes dragged up and down Manu, assessing but giving nothing away. Without speaking, he turned back around and reached up to the shelf above the coffee maker to snag a thick ceramic mug.

"You better have a good explanation for why you're here or I'm going to have to ask you to leave."

One of the slabs of muscle that resided where normal people had shoulders hitched slightly.

"Are ya now?" The drawl of amusement that threaded his voice inflamed Manu.

"Yeah. I am." Manu raised his chin. He was no stranger to a bit of biff on the field, but damned if he didn't try his best to avoid bringing it into his personal life. The thought that this man might have had his meaty paws on Clare though ... Red flashed in front of his eyes.

"I can guarantee the lady of the house isn't interested in having anything further to do with you."

The other man turned slowly, one brow cocked. Leaning back against the benchtop, he folded his arms across his chest.

"Clarity Sage," Hemsworth Lite called out, his eyes never leaving Manu. "Get your butt out here."

From the direction of Clare's bedroom, Manu heard a thump as her feet hit the floor followed by the creak of her door as she rushed into the hall.

Ah, so not asleep then.

"Tex!" Her cry of delight hit the kitchen moments before her body did, and Manu sent up a silent prayer for strength to God because the miniscule cotton boxers and thin t-shirt she was wearing did nothing to conceal the lush curves of her body.

Then she threw herself at the cocky intruder, wrapping her arms tightly around his neck, and Manu prayed again, this time for inner peace because the man had his giant arms wrapped around her back, his nose buried in her hair and a smug smile on his stupidly handsome face that Manu was currently trying to melt off using his Jedi mind trick with wholly murderous intent.

"I thought you were gone for weeks!"

"I am. Just popped back for a quick local job and I'm off again. Be out of here tomorrow." He tucked Clare under a beefy arm and extended his other hand towards Manu. "I'm Theo Miller. We talked over email. This is my apartment."

Manu shook the other man's hand reluctantly. The fact that Clare was still grinning up at Miller with the kind of hero-worshipping smile *he'd* certainly never witnessed did nothing to temper the spike of aggression in him, but he certainly wasn't going to take it out on this bloke, who was after all the reason he wasn't homeless.

"Manu Esera."

"Good to meet you, mate." He grinned down at Clare, and Manu could see the strength of the relationship between them as clearly as if it had been painted on canvas. It stretched between their smiles, golden threads that held them in place, safe and secure that they could count on one another.

Jealousy poured through him, and longing too, at seeing Clare look at someone else like that when it was *his* arm he wanted around her, *his* face he wanted her to smile up into. But he'd never have her, even temporarily. His confession last night had shot that idea in the face as effectively as his move next season would have. He was here for eight weeks, a couple more if the Knights made the finals, and then he'd be gone.

"I thought Clare called you Tex?"

"I did." She grinned up at the blond behemoth adoringly. "It's short for Tech Support. Tex was recruited for the

Army as an intelligence security specialist straight out of high school. He's a genius."

Jesus. She made human beings in a petri dish and was calling this guy a genius. *Doesn't she know anyone with normal intelligence levels? Who might also be ugly?*

"I've got to say," Miller responded, running one hand over the scruff on his face, "I like the idea that there's still someone here looking out for you, Clare Bear."

"Clare doesn't need looking out for," Manu ground out. He'd like to look at her out of her pants, sure, but in terms of self-reliance, Clare made the Unabomber look a bit needy.

Miller looked at him again, long and hard, then he smirked. "No," he replied softly "I guess she doesn't."

"Are you making a coffee?" The woman in question ducked under her landlord's arm and pressed the button on the coffee machine. It whirred to life, filling the air with a heavenly aroma. "Manu, do you want a mocha?" Her tone was stiff, formal. She hadn't looked in his direction once.

"No, thanks." He'd rather chew his arm off than sit here and watch Clare flit around like a happy, relaxed butterfly because of another man. He liked her sour and grumpy and a bit standoffish. That was how she was with *him* and regret that he'd stopped last night rang through his chest. "I'll get one on the way to the stadium."

"You're going now?" She looked at him then, surprised. "I thought you weren't playing until this evening."

"Yeah, well," he shrugged. "Lots to do. Physio and taping and all that. Look, mate." He directed his next words towards Miller. "Sleep in your own bed tonight, yeah? I'll crash on the couch."

He backed away from the whole tempting 'coffee and chocolate and Clare in her tiny, rumpled pyjamas' scene. "See you guys later."

"Good luck," she yelled down the hallway after him, and he closed his eyes against the physical urge to turn around, pick her up, carry her to her bedroom and make her forget the name of any other man she'd ever known in any capacity, celibate or not.

SIX

Manu made it to the stadium in record time, punched in the code and headed straight to the gym, throwing himself on the mats to stretch. *Can't ever be too limber.* The cool, familiar press of the thick pad against his back in the quiet room helped centre him, sanding down the simmering edge of possessiveness that had flared to life when he found Miller in the kitchen.

"Well, well, well, what do we have here?"

He opened his eyes. *Hollis. Perfect.* He shut them again.

"Hey mate, how's it going?"

"Missus kicked me out again." Hollis slumped on a bench nearby. "Why're you here?"

"Just getting a head start. Should be a good game, yeah?"

Hollis snorted. "Fuck the Falcons."

"Fuck the Falcons," Manu echoed absently, hooking his foot into a resistance band and pulling it up until he felt the stretch in his hamstring.

"Fuck you, too."

He opened his eyes, dropped his foot to the floor and sat up.

"What's that?"

"You're not worth the money we're paying you."

Manu took a closer look at the team captain, taking in his red-rimmed eyes and the slackness to his mouth.

"You're drunk."

Hollis snorted, as though being wasted six hours before a professional game was a minor detail. "I'm right, though. You're nothing but a big name with a shit knee. It'll give out again and then we'll be screwed. No replacing you under the current salary cap and a hole in our front row."

Manu pushed aside the twinge of panic at Hollis's mention of his knee. It wasn't perfect, but whose were in this game?

"You've got holes all through your defence, Hollis. I wouldn't worry about the front row. Don't need a lot of scrums when the opposition runs right through your back line. If you were doing your job right, there wouldn't be the spaces there."

Hollis scowled. "You're an arsehole."

"Maybe. But I'm a sober one. Go take a nap. You're supposed to lead us out in six hours and you smell like cheap piss and poor choices."

Hollis flipped him the bird and staggered towards the weights room door as Manu flopped back on the mat. Anger spilled over him, hot and crimson. This wasn't how it was supposed to go. *Twelve years I've been working towards this. Where am I now? On a shit team with a busted knee, pining after a girl who only wants me for sex.*

He lay there for a minute letting the ridiculousness of his life wash through him and breathing in through his nose and out through his mouth the way his soon-to-be sister-in-law, Stella, had instructed him.

He'd been frustrated with the way the accident had hindered him physically, sure. Mentally, the grief had been almost unbearable, the image of his best friend, Tua's, lifeless body haunting him every time he closed his eyes for weeks after. But he'd never really considered the impact of it on his attitude towards sex until now.

He'd made the decision to be celibate in the immediate aftermath, when he was surrounded by white walls, clear tubes and the overwhelming scent of bleach and suffering. His twin justifications - that rebuilding his career needed to be his sole focus and the painful consequences of sex without love - had wrapped around him like the jagged purple scar that painted his left knee. He would do what Tua hadn't been given the chance to do. He would live and breathe and fight for the championship his friend had deserved. Tua had been the very best of them - worked twice as hard on the field, never touched an illicit substance, a true gentleman of the game. Manu owed it to his legacy, to Tua's wife and son, to bring home the championship medal his friend should have had the opportunity to bring home for himself. Women would only distract him, and so he'd decided he would avoid them completely. The embarrassment scored on his father, King Tama's, face every time he visited and saw the tangible results of Aleki's public indiscretions in the bandages that adorned Manu's leg had only cemented that choice. If he could be brought down by the limelight surrounding his brother's love life, he could never risk the fallout of his own relationships impacting his career. But the desire simmering in his blood since he met Clare shone a new light on his choice. He was wild for her, but seven years of abstinence had wound themselves tight into his psyche. He didn't fuck for fun. Aleki had tried that and people had been hurt. *Manu* had been hurt. The evidence still twinged in his knee on cold mornings. There was a child back in Avali without a father because of it.

Breathing out, he let the smell of vinyl and sweat wash away the memories, then he flipped over and started his mountain climbers. If he wanted anything to change, if he wanted to honour Tua's legacy, he had a game to win.

Ten hours later, twenty minutes of which he'd spent sprinting and grappling and being stood on in the dirt, he had to admit winning didn't feel as good as it used to.

Manu eased the door to the apartment open slowly, grateful for the dark shadows of the hallway. The game had ended soon after seven, but he'd hung around the stadium as long as possible, talking shit with Chalmers and seeing the physiotherapist despite having only played the last quarter. The idea of going back to the apartment, back to Clare's awkward avoidance and Tex's wide grin, had held little appeal. The idea of sleeping on the couch even less. Biting back a sigh, he kicked off his shoes and headed down the hallway to the golden glow of the kitchen. A plate sat on the counter covered with one of Clare's reusable beeswax wraps and a yellow Post-It with his name on it. He peeled up the edge of the cover and peeked under.

Lasagne.

What a woman.

He'd eaten at the after-match function, but the heady aroma of rich meat sauce and cheese reached out and wrapped itself around him like a physical embrace. And after the day he'd had, he wasn't going to turn down any kind of comfort.

Unwrapping the plate and slinging it in the microwave,

he pulled a frosty bottle of water from the refrigerator and poured himself a glass while he waited for his meal to heat.

"Hey." The word was soft, but it hit him like a punch.

"Hey." He turned, eyes skimming over Clare from the tangerine tips of her toes to the top of her haphazard bun. And everything in between.

It's still August for God's sake. It's the middle of winter. Why isn't she wearing real pyjamas? Flannel ones. With a high neck.

Clare padded towards him, seemingly oblivious to his thoughts and the effect of her skimpy nightwear on him, and pulled open the cutlery drawer.

"Did you win?"

"Yeah." A pang shot through him at the confirmation she hadn't watched the game. "Thirty-six to twenty-eight."

"That's good." She blinked up at him owlishly as she passed him a knife and fork. "I mean, I guess it is, right?"

Manu huffed out his breath, one corner of his mouth rising. She was too damn cute.

"Yeah, Clare. It's good. We have a game over in Sydney next week and then we're back home for the next two before we have to fly back over. Most of the team's Australian games were played before they signed me, so it cuts down on my travel at least.' He pulled his dinner from the microwave, holding the hot plate by its edges.

"Why do you play in Australia so much?"

"Not enough New Zealand teams to keep a competition going." He shoved a bite of lasagne in and groaned with pleasure. "This is amazing. Did you make this?"

She nodded, her black bun bobbing back and forth with the movement of her head, her gaze never shifting from his mouth.

"Clare?"

She jerked her gaze up to meet his, grey eyes glittering in the low lights of the kitchen.

"You, um." She licked her lips and his breath caught in his chest. "You must be sore from the game. Maybe you shouldn't sleep on the couch tonight."

Time stilled and the air grew thick around him as he paused with his fork halfway to his lips.

"Where should I sleep?" His voice was rough, low.

Small white teeth dented the plush perfection of her lower lip. "You could sleep in my room. Just sleep," she added quickly. "I have a king-sized bed. There's plenty of room."

There would not be plenty of room. A continent would not be enough distance.

"Sure." His voice rasped out. "Just to sleep."

Maybe she didn't think he could see the small, soft smile that flashed across her face in the semi-dark.

"Okay."

"Okay."

Manu wolfed down the rest of the lasagne without tasting it. The layers of meat, cheese and pasta were now burdens to be dealt with as quickly as he was able. Thank goodness he'd been too hungry to add an extra minute on the microwave. A burnt tongue would do him no good tonight.

Slow down, Esera. You're just sleeping, that's all.

The hitch of his heart and the heavy throb behind his balls held fast to their hope despite his rationale.

His cutlery and plate were in the sink the instant the last bite was in his mouth. Swallowing the final forkful with as little chewing as possible, he fixed his gaze on Clare, who had been steadfastly ignoring his attempt at speed-eating.

"I'm pretty beat after the game ..." She let his words

linger in the air and the lack of certainty twisted through him, sharp and unpleasant, before he continued. "If you've changed your mind, it's okay. I'll be fine out here."

Her grey eyes shimmered like molten silver, piercing him through the heart.

"I haven't changed my mind."

Thank the Gods.

He followed her to her bedroom in a lust-soaked haze, paying no attention to anything but the sweet curve of her arse in the golden glow of her bedside lamp as she climbed up onto the large bed. Snuggling down under the covers, she peeked out towards him and Manu felt a sudden burst of protectiveness jolt through him. She looked so sweet and innocent cuddled under a bright red duvet. He was struck by the urge to tell her so but rolled his lips inward to stop the words escaping. The air between them hummed with electricity, low and steady, ready for a spark to ignite it. No way was he going to risk slicing through all of that beautiful yearning energy with clumsy, unwanted words. Instead he shrugged off his official Knights blazer and concentrated on unbuttoning his shirt, focusing on his hands manipulating the thick white cotton lest he throw himself at Clare and ravish her based solely on a bit of eye contact.

The soft intake of her breath as he shrugged the shirt from his shoulders tore at his self-control, but he gritted his teeth and moved on to his belt buckle. He slid his pants down off his legs, taking his socks with them, and stood tall for a second, just in case she wanted a glimpse of him in nothing but his boxer briefs, before easing down onto the plush mattress and pulling the duvet over him.

It might be winter, but the heat they were generating between them was likely to burn him alive.

The lamp clicked off.

Manu lay on his back staring up into the darkness, his breathing as shallow as his thoughts, hot and sticky and entirely inconvenient. Silence stretched through the air, as tangible as a third figure in the bed between them. He slid one arm up under his pillow, only to bump his knuckles against something firm and distinctly inhuman.

"What the—?" The words were unnecessary though, because by the time they were out, his fingers had wrapped around the object and he knew *exactly* what it was.

"What the what?" Clare's voice reached out through the darkness towards him, the husky tenor wrapping around the base of his dick like a fist.

"What," Manu drew the word out slowly, "is a vibrator doing underneath your pillow, Clare?"

SHIT.

It wasn't shame that flooded Clare's body as realisation dawned. There was nothing shameful about masturbation. It was a perfectly natural and healthy thing to do. At the same time though, her *preference* might have been that her unbearably good-looking flatmate did not find her purple vibrator tangled in the sheets where she'd tossed it after cleaning it that afternoon. No, the hot prickle that danced its way down her chest was decidedly unashamed and, problematically, more anticipatory.

Realising Manu was waiting for an answer didn't help.

"Stress relief," she blurted.

"Stress relief." Manu's low voice filled the dark space between them, brushing over her skin and leaving goose-bumps in its wake.

"I'm worried about work."

"Of course you are, sweetheart." He didn't sound convinced, which was fair, because it was a wholly unconvincing lie.

"Would you like to be unburdened?" The question throbbed with intensity, and she couldn't stifle a small moan.

"I-I'm sorry?"

"You are suffering the burden of stress. I can relieve you of that stress. I have the knowledge, the willingness and the necessary equipment."

"Are you talking about the toy?"

"Is that what you want?"

"Maybe?"

"Be sure. Be very sure."

She hesitated. "I thought you didn't do that."

Manu laughed wryly. "Don't worry, Clare. My underwear will stay on. But I can certainly release some of your tension in other ways."

"That ... could be nice."

"Would you like to come, sweetheart? Would that relax you?" A thread of amusement ran through the gravel of his voice like flecks of gold.

"I'm sure it would be very soothing."

"And you would like me to do that for you? With this?"

"Okay."

"Say it, Clare."

She huffed out a small breath as the last of her barriers crumbled under his insistence.

"Yes, Manu. I want you to make me come."

"Thank the gods."

Then his mouth was on her, blazing a trail of fire up her neck, hot and wet. Her nerve endings flared, the combination of desire and ticklishness causing a full body shudder that pressed her against the hard length of him.

Hooking her right leg around his hip, she twisted, pulling him down on top of her into the cradle of her thighs.

Manu groaned, pressing the hard ridge of his erection against the seam of her sleep shorts, and she bucked under him, trying to gain leverage.

"Not so fast *lo'u alofa*," he murmured darkly, leaning down to nip at her jawline.

"Please, Manu," she panted. "I need it."

"You'll get it, sweetheart. Don't worry about that. But half of the fun is the journey. Don't be in such a rush for it to be over that you miss all the good stuff along the way. Now," he paused as he slid one hand between the press of their bodies, "what will I find here?" Slowly, he ran a tantalising finger between her legs and Clare cursed all sleepwear designers that had ever lived.

"Will you be wet for me if I slip my hand inside?"

"Maybe. Yes!" She cried as he scraped his teeth along the curve of her neck. "Yes, I'm wet."

"Why?"

"What?" She arched her neck to look at the silhouette of his head in the darkened room. "Because, during periods of arousal, the Bartholin glands produce additional fluid—"

"Not the science of it, Clare." Manu's head drifted down to her chest and he nudged the thin cotton of her tank top down, exposing her breast. "The reason. Why are you wet right now?"

She hesitated, the words too large and ungainly for her mouth. Then he lapped at her nipple with the broad flat of his tongue, over and over until she was dizzy with need, and the words spilled out like honey - sweet, messy and dangerous.

"Because I want you, goddammit. I want you, Manu."

Her bedside lamp clicked on and in the low golden light he rose above her, his wicked smile and long dark hair making him look like a fallen angel as he smirked down at her.

"You have me, Clare. Now pay attention to what I'm going to do with you."

He sat back on his heels, pulling her shorts and underwear down her legs as he did so. Throwing them behind him, he ran his hands back up her legs, his short nails dragging along her skin and sending shivers ricocheting up her spine until she squirmed under his touch.

"Uh-uh-uh," Manu tutted. "None of that." Using his big palms to secure her at the top of her thighs, his thumbs slid inward to part her folds. Staring down at her, he swallowed hard, then with a look of focused determination on his face, he dipped one thumb inside. Relief surged through Clare immediately, as she arched her back, trying to feel him everywhere.

"Gods, sweetheart." For all the intensity etched into the lines on his face, his voice was ragged. "You're so pretty."

"I bet you say that to all the girls." Her voice wasn't as steady as she'd have liked, either.

His eyes shot up to her face immediately. "No. I don't." Withdrawing his thumb, he plunged two fingers into her and curved them. Clare cried out, curling up as he set an unhurried pace, pumping into her in slow, even strokes as she descended into a dreamlike state of pleasure. Then they were gone, and the cool, blunt tip of the toy was taking their place, sliding through her folds and home, the familiar curve and press of the silicone made novel by the knowledge that Manu was the one working it into her, sliding the toy in and out as she tightened around it. Lying back on the bed, she let the swirling maelstrom inside her build as she closed her eyes and focused on the push and pull of the toy and the blissful stroke across her sweet spot.

Just as her vision started to blur at the edges and she let her lids fall closed, Manu seated the vibrator deep inside her and tilted it so the rabbit-like ears brushed against her clit. Over the heavy saw of her breath, she heard a quiet click, and the ears started to move, vibrating. Three more clicks in quick succession and the stimulation increased, the buzz of the machine in tandem with the buzz in her head. It built and built, the delicious press of the toy inside her, the teasing nudge at her clit and the thick band of Manu's arm across her lower abdomen, simultaneously locking her in place and holding her open as hot waves of desire pulsed through her blood and shimmered behind her lids. The pressure coiled inside her, a carnal corkscrew that tightened with each passing second. Then a whisker-roughened cheek rasped across her nipple and Manu's voice sounded over the lust-soaked pounding of her heart in her ears.

"Let go, lo'u alofa. I've got you."

With a cry she broke, shining shards of light scattering behind her eyelids as pleasure pummelled her like untamed waves in the vastness of the ocean and Manu murmured foreign words to her that sounded like all the promises she never thought she wanted.

SEVEN

Clare was not a morning person. She didn't enjoy the slivers of winter sunshine that snuck through the gaps in her blinds. She was not charmed by the birdsong of early avian risers. And she was most especially displeased by the now-unwelcome presence of a Polynesian prince in her bed. The eager-puppy grin he was giving her was a particularly unspeakable horror. And yet, he spoke.

"Good morning."

Clare grunted.

"Did you sleep well?"

Since he'd brought her to orgasm twice more during the night, once with his mouth and once through dry humping and what Clare assumed was some kind of faerie magic, because surely getting off on dry humping alone wasn't possible, she chose to believe his question was rhetorical.

"Do you need any more stress relieved?"

Good God, the endurance of these pro athletes. It was sickening.

"No, thanks," she replied, trying to temper the growl

that rolled out of her mouth until her first coffee of the morning. "I should be calm until Christmas now."

"Ah, well." She cracked one eye in time to see Manu give her an affable grin. "Surely not Christmas. I foresee a particularly tense time for you in the next couple of months. You'll need all kinds of treatment to address the coming challenges."

Both eyes were open now.

"No, Manu. I won't." She looked at him carefully. Her original plan to exercise a fuck-buddy relationship the length of Manu's lease had been burned to a crisp last night. The orgasms had been amazing, but combined with the sweet nothings he murmured in her ear as he brought her to climax and the warmth of his gaze as he stared at her now, her internal alarms were blaring.

Holy infatuation, Batman.

This was not good. Fuck buddies did not gaze adoringly at her despite her sleep-crusted eyes and bird's-nest hair. Fuck buddies should in fact be gone by the time she opened her eyes. Getting emotionally involved with someone was not on her list of things to do, ever. Emotions were messy, irrational, and above all, left her vulnerable to hurt and rejection. Unacceptable. Clare was no stranger to a beneficial friendship, but the intensity in Manu's dark gaze hinted that trying for that with him would end up with her tangled in more strings than Pinocchio. Better to nip this in the bud now.

"Last night was fun, but it won't happen again." At her words, Manu's open smile faded, hurt creeping into his dark eyes. She injected a little more firmness into her tone. "You're a nice guy, but I think we should just stick to being flatmates for now."

Manu's full lips pressed into a tight line. "You don't think you need my help anymore?"

"Our original agreement can still stand," she hedged. "I value your advice. But if you're not comfortable helping me after this, I understand. You're a busy guy, after all. Lots of ball throwing and stuff to do." She gestured weakly with her hand, having absolutely no idea what kind of things this league player did on a regular basis except turn her on.

Manu laughed, low and bitter. Something in Clare's stomach dropped at hearing such a caustic sound coming from a man with the personality of a golden retriever. "Never let it be said I am not a team player. We will resume lessons on Tuesday." He threw back the covers, exposing acres of warm bronze skin as he sat and gathered up the clothes he'd discarded the night before. Shrugging into them, he stood and exited the room swiftly, without another glance at her.

She winced as her bedroom door closed firmly behind him, then again at the muffled bang of the apartment's front door seconds later. Kicking off her own portion of the duvet, she wrapped herself in her cuddly robe and went in search of coffee.

Irritation prickled under her skin as she moved around the kitchen pulling a clean mug from the dishwasher and sifting through the coffee capsules in the pantry to find the darkest roast. The image of Manu's puppy dog eyes poked at the edges of her subconscious.

What does he want from me? He knows I'm not good at this shit. And people think women have trouble separating sex and emotions.

She growled softly into the pantry.

"Woah. Sounds like your train's pulling into Frustration Station over there." Tex's easy drawl raked over her.

"I'm not frustrated," she snarled, sounding extremely frustrated even to her own ears. "I just don't understand why we don't have any bloody biscuits in this whole bloody flat."

Smirking, Tex pulled a chair from the dining nook over to the pantry and elbowed her gently out of the way so he could stand on it. He rummaged around at the back of the top shelf, and a packet of chocolate digestives magically dropped from the sky. She caught them instinctively, the crinkle of the packet like music to her ears.

"You're a legend, Tex."

"Make us a cup of tea then."

She turned, holding half a digestive by her teeth, and flicked the switch on the kettle before shoving another biscuit into her mouth while ignoring the crumbs that dropped onto her robe-covered boobs.

"So ..."

She turned to see Tex leaning against the closed pantry doors, jeans low-slung, arms folded across his bare chest, looking every inch like an untamed male model and a pain in her arse.

"So what?"

"No Manu this morning?"

She gritted her teeth. "Guess not."

"You scare him away with your big, bad bitch act?" Tex's voice danced with amusement.

Clare levelled Death Glare Number Three at her flat-mate. No warm up, straight to the big guns.

"What makes you think that?"

"Time. History. Experience. The number of gentle souls I've had to counsel on that couch over there after you left them limp and weeping once you were done with them." Tex sighed dramatically, running a hand over his stubble. "It's enough to make a man want to stay single forever."

"I don't think you're in any danger of being snatched up soon. You look like a wildebeest. Shaving wouldn't hurt. You can use my razor if you want. I did my bikini area with it a couple of days ago, but since that's probably the closest you'll come to a vulva in the next year, I'm sure you won't mind."

Tex threw back his head in laughter while she continued to glare at him through narrowed eyes. Behind her, the kettle reached boiling point in a show of solidarity.

"Oh, Clare Bear. What on earth are we going to do with you?" Tex moved towards her and flicked open the drawer that housed his tea collection. Pulling out a tin of loose-leaf green and jasmine - *fricking health nut* - he scooped some into a steeper and handed it to her. She plonked it into a mug just hard enough for a couple of the leaves to fall out of the join.

Good. See how he liked his tea with floaties in it.

She poured the hot water in and shoved the mug down the counter towards her foster brother, then made her own coffee, as short and sharp as the settings would allow.

Black. Like my heart.

She carted it to the couch with her precious biscuits.

Tex folded himself on the opposite end of the sectional and motioned for the packet.

"How is your love life going, anyway?" She frowned over the rim of her mug at him. "Any special ladies or lads missing you at the moment?"

Tex rolled his head back against the back of the couch, blond hair flopping over his eyes. "Ah, you know how it is, Clare Bear. They always want to come, but they never want to leave."

"Slut," she snorted teasingly, and he shot her a grin that lit his hazel eyes and wiped the years from his face. Suddenly they were eleven and thirteen again, catching each other's eyes in the Pritchetts' living room, while the blood relatives fought around them, and sharing in the knowledge that as the token foster kids none of it was their problem. Tex had been her lifeline when she arrived at the Pritchetts', and when he'd been adopted by another family two years later, she'd been devastated, especially when the Pritchetts tossed her back into the system, but Tex had stayed in touch all the way through her adolescence. New Zealand didn't have orphanages like many other countries, so he'd bought her her very first cell phone as a way for them to keep in touch as she was bounced between short- and long-term fostering. When she'd aged out, she'd moved in with him while she attended university.

"Nah, not much to tell," Tex continued, his face settling back into the mask of responsibility he wore all too often nowadays. "I've been focusing on work, looking more at the private sector recently."

"You're leaving the army?" Surprise coloured her voice. Tex had been headhunted for his computer skills while still at high school and as far as she knew had never shown any indication that he was unsatisfied with his choice.

"I'm thinking about it." He shifted uncomfortably on the couch. "Lots of rich people need personal cyber security. I've been talking to my mate Liam about it. Might be time to see what else the world outside of Her Majesty's Service has to offer."

"Get that money." She sipped her coffee. "Manu's been helping me try to strengthen my application for Trish's position. Applications will open in late October so there's only a few weeks left."

Tex smirked at her over his tea. "Is that all he's helping you with?"

"Shut up."

"I'm serious, Clare." He lowered his mug and looked at her. "He seems like a nice guy. You can't shut everyone out forever. You deserve to be happy."

"I am happy."

Tex smiled softly. "If you say so."

They fell into silence, passing the chocolate biscuits back and forth, and Clare tried very hard to ignore the icy sense of foreboding creeping down her arms.

THIS PLACE AGAIN.

Given the amount of time Manu was spending at the Knights' training facility, the front office could have saved themselves the trouble of subletting Tex's apartment bedroom and just thrown a blanket down on the practice pads for him. Bypassing the gym, he headed straight for the pool. Stripping down to his underwear, he dove in, the cool water closing over his head like hands in prayer. Surfacing halfway down the lane, he rolled onto his back and kicked lazily, the back and sides of his head still submerged. The combination of the quiet space and the refreshing water relaxed his body and his mind, loosening his tight muscles and gnarled thoughts so he could focus on them one by one.

You're a busy guy. Lots of ball throwing to do. Clare's words echoed in his head, the flat vowels of her New Zealand accent stretching the words and imbuing them with a meaning he couldn't quite decipher. Was it sarcasm, the way his brother, Aleki, sometimes joked about his career out of a misplaced sense of guilt? Or something else? Maybe

Clare was as awkward about their differences as she was about small talk. Maybe this *was* her version of small talk. Or maybe she just didn't understand? Another academic up on her high horse of funding jealousy and the entertainment appeal of so-called Neanderthal sports.

"*Cowabunga!*" The distorted cry cut through the water that covered Manu's ears moments before the splash rocked him, shunting his body sideways and raining water down on his face.

Spluttering, he rolled upright, treading water as Chalmers popped up beside him with a manic grin.

"Finn, you idiot. Are you ever going to grow up?"

He and Finn both turned towards the voice. A willowy redhead stood at the side of the pool with hands on her hips as she gazed at Chalmers with irritation.

"Yes, dear. Any day now," the fullback called back as he pushed his hair back from his face. "Cara, meet Manu. He's a new recruit who's going to take us to the finals." The redhead snorted, but Chalmers ignored her. "Manu, this is Cara. She only hangs around me so I'll take her out to eat."

"Which you promised me forty-five minutes ago," Cara responded tartly. "Nice to meet you, Manu," she offered in a kinder tone.

"Likewise." Manu nodded.

"Give us twenty minutes for aqua jogging and I'll feed you immediately after," Finn called up. Rolling her eyes, Cara pulled an e-reader from her tote bag and headed to the in-built seating that ran the length of the pool.

Manu tried not to think about how eye-rolling and e-readers were fast becoming turn-ons for him, especially as he watched how Chalmers' eyes tracked Cara's retreat. Fortunately, in his case it seemed to be limited to angry dark-haired scientists.

"She seems nice," Manu commented, deliberately keeping his tone mild as they turned towards the end of the lane and began jogging through the chest-deep water.

"Hmmm," Finn intoned, flashing him a suspicious glance. "She is. Too nice for her own good." At Manu's quizzical look, he sighed. "She got stood up last night by a guy she's been dating. I'm going to take her to brunch and fill her full of bacon and mimosas until she doesn't care anymore."

"What a dick," Manu declared, as they turned at the end of the lane. "Doesn't take much to flick off a text and say you can't make it."

"Right?" Chalmers shook his head. "These kids today, no respect."

Since Chalmers was only about twenty-four himself, Manu ignored that bit.

"What about you, Esera? Been tearing it up with the ladies? Plying them with kava? Promising them trips back to your island paradise?" Chalmers voice was light, teasing. Manu knew his reputation for clean living was a contrast to much of the scandalous environment of professional sports. The Knights' rookie centre, Rangi Katu, had made more televised apologies since being signed eight months ago than Manu had in his entire career.

"Not much chance of that I'm afraid," he replied. "It's a full-time job trying to keep this team afloat."

"No time for dillydallying with the fairer sex?" Chalmers waggled his eyebrows in a ridiculous Groucho Marx impression and Manu laughed.

"Not a second to spare. The only woman I even see is my flatmate."

"What's she like?" They reached the other end of the lane and turned again.

"She's brilliant. She's a scientist, helps make IVF babies. I'm helping her try and get a promotion at the moment." *Funny as fuck. Smells like lemons. Comes around my hand like a geyser.* He left his final thoughts out, but something must have played across his face because Chalmers had stopped jogging and was looking at him a bit too closely.

"You should invite her to a game," the younger man suggested. "She could sit up in the box with all the WAGS and Cara."

"I don't think it's her kind of thing," Manu admitted hesitantly. "I get the feeling she's one of those girls who doesn't think much of the job."

"Bullshit. All girls love a pro athlete." Chalmers started jogging again. "If she's not into it yet, it's just because she hasn't seen you play. Once she gets a load of those thighs in action, she'll be a fan for life."

Manu coughed, discomfort rising in his chest. But hell, he wasn't one for angst and getting this out might make him feel better. "She, um, she's seen the thighs actually. Not on the field, but she's had some experience in that area."

"Reeeeeally?" Finn sounded delighted. "And she's still not sure she wants to commit herself to an eighty minute game cheering you on?"

"She doesn't want to commit to anything," Manu grumbled, doing his best not to sound petulant, but he could hear the hurt underpinning his words all too clearly. "Not even a friends with benefits scenario." In fairness, the benefits he was offering might not be the full-scale package, but there was no need for Chalmers to know that. At times like this, he missed Aleki. His brother would know what to say. Therapy had only made Aleki better at problem-solving.

"Is that what you want?"

"I don't know, man." Manu added a couple of angry

strokes through the water, the cool sluice of liquid tempering the hot flush of frustration under his skin. "I know that I like her. But she told me just this morning in bed that she wasn't interested. I have to respect that. Besides, this contract isn't permanent, our housing situation isn't permanent. You know how this game goes. I could be traded tomorrow."

"You could. But guys who do what we do know better than most that if you want something you have to go after it."

"Is that what you would do?"

Chalmers slid his gaze towards the stand where Cara sat reading. "It's not always that easy."

"No, it's not," Manu agreed. Thoughts clicked over in his head. "Do you think I should send her flowers to say sorry if I overstepped?"

"Oh my God." They both started as a new voice rang out. "Do not do that."

"Uh, Cara." Finn's voice was tentative. "I'm not sure you got the full story there."

Cara shot him an exasperated look. "Do you have any idea how high these ceilings are, Finn? How well sound travels? I heard every word." She turned her attention to Manu. "Look, this girl, she's smart, yes?" Manu nodded. "Then she's thought this through. She's probably done a pros and cons list. And despite what Finn thinks" - she shot him a dark glare - "not every girl is frothing at the mouth to be reduced to WAG-status in a sport where sex scandals and off-field bar fights are rampant. What did she say exactly?"

Manu searched his brain. "That I'm a nice guy. And that we should just stick to being flatmates."

"Then that's how you treat her. Would you send a male

flatmate flowers to apologise for overstepping if you ate the last of his yogurt?"

"No."

"No. So don't send them to her. Pull back, give her some space, make friendly conversation and do as much as you can to get back to how things were before you guys had your adult fun-times. That's what a nice guy would do." She folded her arms over her chest. "Finn, I'm starving. Take me to pancakes before I dump you as a friend and you have to get all your advice from this guy."

"Yes, dear." Finn scrambled up the ladder like a spider monkey before looking back down at Manu in the water. "By the way, that's what I was going to say."

He darted away from the tide of water Manu splashed at him, his laughter echoing up to the rafters.

EIGHT

The Knights' training pitch gleamed in the winter sunlight, a green oasis in the middle of grey stadium seating. Clare shifted uncomfortably on the sidelines, her left hand automatically going to the St Christopher's necklace at her throat. From the corner of her eye, she saw Manu glance at her.

"You okay, there?"

The deep rumble of his voice was edged with amusement, which she *did not appreciate* considering he had whisked her out of bed at some ungodly hour. He had then gently steered her towards the shower, all while promising her a bright opportunity to hone her small-talk skills and the largest coffee known to man. Admittedly, the coffee was enormous, the size of her head. Strong and black and just hot enough to scald the tip of her tongue on the first sip. She cradled her takeaway cup to her now, wrapping her fingers around the warmth as she replied.

"Mmm hmmm."

She caught Manu's grin in her peripheral vision before he turned and surveyed the field.

"So, with a charity practice like this, the kids come in with their parents and the charity workers and we run a few light drills with them. There's a little pick-up game for those that are strong enough, but for the most part it's just about the kids coming in, spending a bit of time with us and getting some merchandise."

"Which charity are you working with today?"

"Today we've got the Youth Athletes from the Special Olympics programme coming in. It's gonna be great." Manu's smile stretched wider, his dark eyes crinkling at the corners. He radiated positivity the way the sun radiated light.

"Okay." She heard the uncertainty in her voice and hated it. Clare Trescott was not a weakling. She was born of struggle and sacrifice, and the idea of being surrounded by a bunch of strapping sportsmen playing nice with kiddies in the morning sun should not fill her with the hot prickle of anxiety. Even after a decade out of the system, meeting new people in a group setting triggered something deep inside her. She was twenty-eight, a professional, a functioning member of society, dammit. Not a scared little girl waiting for the judgement of others to find her worthy. Once again, a flare of anger rushed through her stomach at the way the foster system operated - twisting children into artificial moulds to appeal to families like a sick *Bachelor*-style game.

Manu clapped a huge hand on her shoulder. He'd been full of pal-style gestures since their awkward encounter last Sunday morning - shooting her the thumbs up when she asked him a question, leaving her notes if he was going to be late, even calling her 'bro' in a text. She wasn't sure what was going on, but anything was better than the sad puppy eyes of Sunday so she wasn't questioning it.

"Don't worry, Clare. I got you a babysitter." He raised

his hand and a man who looked like he should be gracing the front of romance novels with his shaggy, dark blond hair, cut-glass jaw and the body of a young Adonis came jogging towards them, trailed by a tall redheaded woman.

"Hey." The new guy gave Manu a complicated handshake, raking his eyes over Clare with unabashed curiosity.

"Finn, this is Clare. Clare, this is Finn Chalmers and Cara." Manu made introductions as the woman joined them. She smiled warmly and held out her hand.

"Cara Holt."

Clare shook it firmly. "Clare Trescott."

"Nice to meet you, Clare." Cara eyed the men over the rims of her mirrored aviators. "We're going up into the stands to talk about you and eat cheese." She lifted a woven tote bag. "Have fun, boys."

Manu caught Clare's eye and smiled encouragingly at her. "Be gentle with her, Cara," he said to the other woman, who laughed in response.

"Always."

Clare trailed behind Cara up the first few concrete steps of stadium seating. They settled into a row and Cara unpacked a range of cheese out of her tote, along with crackers, quince paste, a small board and a cheese knife. She arranged them on the spare seat between them as Clare looked on impressed.

"So," Cara began, slicing off a hunk of smoked gouda. "Manu said you're a scientist?"

"Reproductive science," Clare responded, accepting a loaded cracker. "What do you do?"

"I'm a preschool teacher," Cara replied. "You make 'em, I educate 'em."

Clare spent the next hour chatting with Cara, discussing their favourite streaming shows and true crime podcasts. Her nerves evaporated as they chatted - the other woman was funny and interesting. At one point, a riot of young people poured out of the stadium tunnel and flooded onto the field, swarming Manu, Finn and the other Knights players as they looked on.

Clare caught Manu's eye as he lifted one young man onto his shoulders, and he waved. The kid on his shoulders did the same, his arm swinging in a wide, joyful arc against the blue sky. Happiness bubbled up in Clare as she waved back, laughing as Manu turned away and galloped off with his young charge clutching his braids like reins.

She turned back to the cheeseboard and caught Cara staring at her.

"What? Do I have crumbs on my face?" She swiped at her mouth.

"Nope. Let's go down and say hi."

Apprehension slid through Clare. "I don't think we can do that." *I don't want to do that.* She'd come, she'd talked to Cara without scaring her off. The swarm of people on the field was an unknown quantity. Too many people, too much potential for her to say the wrong thing, do the wrong thing, embarrass Manu or herself.

"Sure we can. Look at all the women over there." Cara gestured towards a group on the sidelines - a mix of parents and carers, a few Cara had pointed out already as being WAGs or Knights staff. Clare reluctantly followed her down the stairs and onto the sidelines, pausing at the edge of the group as Cara greeted some of the others warmly.

"Woah, woah, woah, little buddy." Manu jogged to a stop beside her, but his attention was focused on the boy on his shoulders. "Time for a rest by this pretty lady here."

"I'm Tim," his rider announced loudly, staring down at

Clare. "I have Down Syndrome and I'm going to win a gold medal in swimming someday. This is my horse, Manu."

"Hi, Tim," Clare said, shielding her eyes as she looked up at him. "I'm Clare. What's your favourite swimming event?"

"I like backstroke. Put me down, horsie," Tim commanded, and Clare hid a smile as Manu dropped gently to his knees and helped the boy clamber down. "I need some water. You can stay here."

Manu's gaze followed Tim as he wandered into the small crowd and tugged on the arm of a woman who looked to be in her early thirties.

"A man who knows what he wants. I like it." He turned towards Clare. "How are you going?"

"Good," she replied, a little surprised to realise it was the truth. "Cara's really nice. Excellent taste in cheese."

"An essential quality," Manu acknowledged with a tilt of his head.

"How are you?"

"So good. This is one of the best parts of what we do," he said, turning to look out over the field where players were taking selfies with the young athletes, signing jerseys and hats, and dishing out high fives. 'Seeing these kids, knowing that just talking to them or spending time with them can make them light up? It's the same feeling as winning a game."

Softened by her successful navigation of social niceties and a belly full of cheese, she stared up at Manu and one of the walls she'd painstakingly built around her heart cracked.

Shit.

"SHIT."

Manu stared down at his soaked T-shirt. One day he would learn to do the dishes without looking like he'd been free-diving, but today was not that day. Sighing, he stripped it off over his head.

"Hey, Manu, have you—" Clare's voice trailed off as she came to a halt after rounding the refrigerator.

He waited a beat, observing how her eyes darted across his chest and over the bands of the tattoo on his left arm.

"Have I ..." he prompted when no other words were forthcoming. He hadn't expected to see her. She'd disappeared to her room as soon as they got back from the stadium and hadn't even come out for dinner.

"Huh?"

"Have I what?"

"Oh!" Clare shook her head slightly. "Have you seen my e-reader? I thought it was in my room but I can't find it."

Warmth rose in his cheeks. "It's by the TV. I moved it when I was tidying up." He'd moved it. And he'd looked at it. The screen had flashed to life when he'd knocked a button and the memory of the page he'd seen ran through his mind and sent heat spiralling down to settle heavily between his thighs.

"Oh, okay. Thanks." She gave him a quick, tight smile and moved to pick it up. "See you tomorrow."

"See you." His strangled voice sounded unfamiliar to his own ears as he watched her leave, her purple-tipped fingers wrapped around the device.

Get a grip, man. Going off to her room to read about a governess being plundered by a neighbouring rake is clearly a sign that she'd rather spend time having fun by herself than with you.

The mental reminder did nothing to settle him as he

closed his eyes. Clare's round face popped into his mind, only this time she was wearing a yellow corseted dress that pushed her boobs up towards her chin. His groan echoed audibly in the open-plan space, and he pressed his palm against the ridge in his jeans.

His phone pinged and he reluctantly moved his hand to his back pocket to fish it out.

Are you OK? Heard a weird sound.

Of course she had. Because he was palming his dick in the middle of their shared living space like a boundary-stomping arsehole.

All good, he typed back. *What are you reading?*

Three little dots appeared, then disappeared, then returned.

A book about Victorian etiquette.

Right. So, governess-plundering it was.

Are you enjoying it?

It's adequate.

Manu chuckled and pressed the call button.

"Hello?" Clare sounded a little winded, and courage burned through him like whiskey at the thought of what activities might be using up her energy.

"Is that Victorian etiquette book not quite up to your standards, Clare?"

"I've read better."

"I could give you better." The words were out before he could stop them. He saw them hanging in the air in front of him and the desire to stop time, to shove them back down inside him, was so potent it was like a hand around his throat.

"What?" Her voice was almost a whisper now, hesitancy softening the edges of her usually crisp speech.

"I could ... I could tell you a better story. If you wanted."

"Could you now?"

His hand was back on his dick, soft strokes through the thick denim. Just removed enough from his skin to feel like the hand could be someone else's. To feel like it could be hers.

"Yes."

"Go on then."

"It's about a governess. And a rake."

"Manu." Delight and reproach struggled for dominance in her tone. "Have you been snooping?"

"Of course not. I'm a big *Bridgerton* fan."

"Mmmmm." She didn't believe him and he didn't care.

"There's a ball." Horniness made him bold. "She's upstairs, the children are asleep, and she's thinking about all the fun she's missing out on below. He comes up the stairs looking for a bit of peace and quiet."

"Does he find it?"

"He does not. Do you know what he finds instead?"

"Her?"

"Her." Manu moved towards the couch and lowered himself down, flicking open the button fly of his jeans as he did so. "What do you think she's doing, Clare?" He eased his hand inside his underwear.

"I think ... I think she's in the dark, in her room. And I think he walks in by mistake."

"Ah. And what would etiquette call for in that case?"

"He should, uh, apologise, and leave."

"And is that what our rake does, Clare?"

Her breath hitched, the sound echoing through Manu's phone, and he gripped himself tightly, revelling in the shaky timbre of her words.

"No."

"What do I do?"

She didn't miss the character change. "You, um, you close the door. You move closer.'

"To who?"

"To me."

"And what do you do?"

"I wait. I wait to see what you do."

"What do you think I do?"

"I think you get on your knees."

Sweet holy gods, yes. He squeezed his dick so hard he almost blacked out.

"And then?" Was that his voice? It was ... strained. Very, very strained.

"And then you lift up my skirts. Slowly. You don't say anything. You just look at me and push them up over my knees."

"Watching you."

"Watching me. Watching me watch you."

"Your legs are so soft." He could see them now, pale and sweet in the light of the moon. Fabric brushed against the top of her thighs, hiding her from his view. Nothing but the seduction of the shadows. "Part them for me."

Clare's small sigh echoed, a little mewl that wrapped around him and he thrust into his fist, desperate for another.

"I'm going to touch you now."

"Yes please."

In his mind he inched the skirt up, baring her to the waist. She was wearing a lace thong, which was probably all wrong, but fuck it, he didn't care, because he pushed it to the side and he could see her now. She was perfect, the plump swell of her lips, as soft as rose petals. He ran his thumb along her crease and slipped in between. Spreading the honey of her arousal up in slow strokes, brushing against the perfect jewel of her clit, once, twice, three times.

"You're so soft, lo'u alofa. You're so soft and wet and lovely and mine."

"Manu." Her voice was desperate now, in his ear and in his mind. "Manu, please."

"Do you need it baby? Do you need me?" He was lost to the fantasy, pre-come pouring from his tip, slicking his hand's journey as he stroked himself, the buzz of arousal blurring the edges of his mind until the only thing he could see or hear was Clare, opened for him, wet and needy and panting in his ear. "Fuck, baby, that's it. Come on my fingers."

"Manu!" He heard her cry in stereo, coming from the phone and the hallway at the same time. "Jesus fucking Christ, you feel so good." A pause, a gasp, and then a whining sound that rose and shuddered through the air, tearing through him with the same force as his orgasm that hit his stomach in warm licks the instant he realised she was coming for him, with nothing but their words and imaginations from half an apartment away.

He groaned into the phone as the aftershocks zinged through him, three long, wet pulls to drain every last drop and gods help him if he didn't imagine it was her mouth while he did it.

"Clare?" Five miles of unpaved island roads, that's what he sounded like. *That's what she's done to me.*

"Yeah?"

"You have sweet dreams now."

He thumbed his phone off before she could say anything, before she could reach inside while he was gasping and vulnerable and tear him to pieces while he lay spent at her feet. Then he stared into the darkness and let his satisfaction roll through him in slow sticky waves.

NINE

Manu gasped, pulling in desperate slugs of oxygen that burned down his oesophagus and into his waiting lungs. Sweat ran down into his eyes and he swiped at it with a grass-covered hand. The ragged sounds of his teammates breathing echoed in the crisp winter air as they gathered in the in-goal area, the pain of the sprint exercises driving even the fittest players to exhaustion.

"Fuck me," Chalmers panted, dropping his hands to his knees as he came up beside Manu. "Who pissed in Harro's cornflakes this morning?"

Manu grunted in response, gratefully catching the water bottle that came flying towards him from one of the coaching staff who had descended on the desperate group.

Even the sweet relief of water didn't cool the burning sensation in his chest. He hadn't seen Clare in person since their X-rated phone call and the fact that she was clearly avoiding him sat uncomfortably

"Manu." He straightened as his name was called across the field.

"Yes, Coach?"

Harro swaggered over, trusty tablet clutched to his barrel chest. "You're looking good out there. I'm going to start you on Saturday."

Dizzying relief flowed through him. "Thank you, Coach. I appreciate it."

"Humph." Harro replied, turning on his heel.

He caught Chalmers eye and the other man reached over for a high five. "Finals, here we come, baby."

The reminder settled Manu. He'd lost his mind a little over Clare Trescott and her tiny pyjamas and homemade lasagne and kind encounters with Special Olympian kids. But that had to stop. He didn't have Aleki's talent for being taken seriously. He had now what he'd always had, a talent for sports and for the push that came with grinding his way to a higher tier, a greater outcome every year. That was how he served his people. It was how he paid tribute to Tua's memory. To forget his purpose was to dishonour himself, his friend and his country. The only thing he needed to be focusing on was how he could get the Knights to the quarter-finals.

Ambition cut through Manu fiercely, spilling out of his mouth in a hard wave. "I need us to get there."

Chalmers looked up at him from the downward dog he'd sunk into. "Me too, brother. Me too." He paused. "What are you doing after this?"

Manu straightened and stretched upwards, his fingers linked loosely as he felt the sweet pop of something in his back settle back into its proper place. "Weights until noon, then home. Not a lot going on in my life right now."

"Want to come to mine?" Finn peered up at him from a triangle stretch. "Play a little Call of Duty, watch some old Bulls tapes? Talk shit about Hollis?"

Manu laughed, his breath puffing out in front of him. "Sounds good. Can I catch a ride with you?"

"You didn't bring your car today?"

"Nah." Manu shifted slightly on his feet, clenching the muscles around his knee reflexively. "I don't drive." Every time he got near a steering wheel he seized up, the memories bombarding him. Voices shouting, the flash of cameras popping behind his eyes, the grumble of an engine and then pain, so much pain. Sweat that had nothing to do with their cardio workout popped up along his hairline.

After practice finished in a brutal round of calisthenics, Manu pulled his phone from his locker and fired off a quick text to Clare.

It's Tuesday. Practice tonight.

He shoved his phone in his bag and headed to the shower, determined not to check for a response. It didn't matter if she replied or not. In fact, it was probably better if she didn't. He could spend his evening doing extra bodyweight training in his room or reviewing play footage.

He made it until his butt hit the passenger seat in Finn's car before he checked his phone. No reply. Still no reply once they got to Finn's and he trounced Manu thoroughly through three rounds of Playstation battles. No reply on the drive home or while he ate his afternoon snack of three hard-boiled eggs, carrots and hummus.

He was still waiting for a reply at seven, when a loud thump sounded from the direction of the apartment's front door. Impatience twanged at Manu's nerves - if it was just kids messing about he was going to be severely pissed off. However, when he swung the door open, he was greeted with the sight of Clare draped over a redheaded giant who looked like he'd be more at home trying to liberate medieval Scotland than wrangling a pocket sized pinup in an inner city hallway. Her keys, identified by her stuffed-sperm keyring, were on the floor in front of them.

"Oh, thank God," William Wallace said. "Here, take your woman." He thrust a loose-limbed Clare at Manu, who caught her instinctively.

"You're home," she declared loudly, peering up into his face with an unfocused gaze.

"I am." Manu looked up at her companion. "I'm her flatmate."

"I'm Jeremy. We work together." He grimaced. "She's had a bit of a shit day. I thought a couple of drinks might cheer her up, but they just appear to have put her on her arse."

Clare wound her arms around Manu, cuddling into his chest. The smell of lemons hit him like a two-by-four and he sucked air in like he was dying, wrapping his own arm around the soft press of her body.

"It was *awful*." Her words were slightly slurred, but they didn't mask the tremble in her voice.

He glanced at Jeremy. "Has she eaten?"

"I had a protein bar for lunch." Clare assured him earnestly.

"That was a Snickers."

"Peanuts have protein in them, Jeremy!"

Manu sighed. "It's okay, sweetheart. I'll make you some toast."

"I fucking love toast."

"I'm sure you do." He looked up at the other man. "Thank you for bringing her home safely."

"No worries. Tell her I'll give her a call in the morning."

Manu nodded and shut the door. He bent at the waist so he could tuck a shoulder under Clare's armpit and steered her down the hallway towards the living area.

Depositing her carefully on the couch, he covered her with the big cream blanket she seemed to favour and headed towards the kitchen area.

"Life is so unfair, y'know?" Clare's plaintive voice reached him as he dropped two pieces of bread in the toaster and pushed the lever down.

"How so?"

"I had this patient today. Young guy, early twenties. Seemed really nice. He's just been diagnosed with leukaemia. He wanted to freeze his sperm so he could have babies later after his treatment." Her voice hitched. "I checked them after he gave his sample. They were all dead. All of them." On the last word, her voice broke and Manu abandoned the toaster for the couch, wrapping his arms around Clare as sobs racked her body and she clung to him for dear life.

Eventually her shudders calmed and she leaned back. He let her go but linked their fingers and rested their joined hands on the blanket that swaddled her.

"Sorry for snotting all over your shirt," she said, her vowels loose and round.

"Don't worry about it," he responded, leaning in to drop a soft kiss on her forehead.

"Can I have some toast now please?" Clare offered him a weak smile, not a trace of it reaching her red-rimmed eyes.

He ran his thumb over hers gently, trying to comfort her without words. "Sure thing."

Heading for the kitchen area, he tossed the cold toast in the bin and popped two more down to cook. Digging in the fridge and pantry, he assembled his supplies, ready to slather them on as soon as the toast pinged upwards. He might limit his own diet throughout the season, but there wasn't a Pacific Island man alive who didn't know how to prepare comfort food like a pro. Food played a central role in Avali - at celebrations, village meetings, social outings and at falelauasiga, the funeral processes. His own mother's funeral was one of his earliest memories - sitting next to Aleki, wearing a lavalava and long-sleeved white shirt that rubbed at his neck while he demolished keke saiga, traditional onion biscuits, with the innocence of a child who didn't truly understand what was happening in his world. He still couldn't eat keke saiga now. At least there was less chance of today's trauma ruining peanut-butter-and-Nutella toast for Clare. Satisfied with his offering, he piled it all onto a plate and turned back towards the living area, only to see her slumped over, her beautiful tear-streaked face squashed into the leather as she slept.

CLARE CLAMBERED out of sleep a step at a time. First the consciousness, then the battle to open one eyelid, then the other. Groaning, she turned her head, only to have her cheek brush against the soft wool of her favourite blanket. The television glowed in the dark of the room, a league game in full obnoxious colour but blessedly silent.

"Hey there." Manu's voice was soft, brushing over her like a caress, even as her head began to pound.

"What time is it?" Clare responded.

"Just after nine. Do you still want toast? This stuff has gone cold but I can make some more. I ordered Chinese earlier as well in case you want that?"

"Maybe some noodles?"

He dished her up a bowl of noodles with some kung-pao chicken on the side and settled in next to her when she sat up to reach for it. He stretched an arm along the back of the couch, and she leaned back towards him as she forked food into her mouth, not touching exactly, but the warmth was a solid presence behind her.

"Thanks for the food."

"No worries. There's water and painkillers on the table as well." Manu watched her intently, his dark eyes glittering in the shadows of the room and heat crept into her cheeks even as she tried to focus on the food. "How are you feeling?"

"Shitty."

"Yeah." He ghosted a hand across her hair. "Emotionally or physically?"

"Both."

"Want to hear a joke?"

"'Kay."

"An Irishman walks out of a bar." He stopped, and she peered up at him over her bowl, waiting for the punchline.

"That's it. That's the joke."

She snorted softly, a reluctant smile pulling at her lips. "That's terrible."

"You try one then."

She searched her brain as she poked through her food for a chunk of chicken.

"Okay, what do you call a fake noodle?"

He waited, eyes on her.

"An im-pasta."

Manu let out a groan, painting the air around him with the rich brush of his accent.

"Clare Trescott, I cede to you in horrible jokes. You have defeated me."

She bowed her head as graciously as she could with her mouth full.

"You should tell those sort of jokes at work. You'd be promoted in no time."

The mention of work threw up memories of her day, the microscopic image of dead sperm in a petri dish, and tears pricked behind her eyes, sharp and sour.

"Tell me something nice. Tell me about Tex," Manu said quickly, and she would have smiled at the panic in his eyes if she wasn't such a raw aching nerve right now. "How did you meet him?"

She pressed her lips together, the memory slicing through her like a blade, as tangible as ever. She leant down to place her bowl on the floor and pulled the blanket further up around her shoulders, letting her head fall back against the press of Manu's forearm when she sat back up.

"He was my foster brother," she said quietly. "I got placed with the Pritchetts when I was eleven. Tex's mother was an addict, and he lived with his grandmother until she died when he was thirteen. They were his first foster family. His only one. The Pritchetts had three biological children but they wanted to foster as well. They were very big in their church and I think that had a lot to do with it. So I arrived, and all of the bio kids were nice enough, but they were quite a bit older than us and not really interested in these tagalong kids that had been added to their family for show. The oldest two were already at university. Tex was the only one who was really interested in me. He taught me how to play poker and chess and we'd go to the library on Saturdays to read books together and argue about them."

"And you guys stayed together the whole time?"

Her smile faded. "No. No, two years after I arrived, Tex was adopted by an older couple. So he left. I was thirteen and I didn't take it very well. The Pritchetts were having some marriage trouble, their youngest kid was out of the house and Tex was gone, so it was just me and the parents. They didn't really want an angsty teenager without a buffer, so they sent me back into the system. But Tex stayed in touch. His adoptive parents ask me over for Christmas and stuff each year, but I'm not really big on the family environment."

Manu stroked his thumb across the soft skin at the back of her neck.

"And you weren't adopted?'

"No. After the Pritchetts, I bounced around emergency foster care for a few months, then a year with the Wipanis and then the Lambs. I thought they might be it for me. They seemed really nice. They had a daughter my age and paid for me to go to private school. Then Madison wrote off the Beemer when we were coming back from the mall one day and she told them I was driving. Bye-bye to the Lambs." Her voice was wry, but the vulnerability rang through like a gong.

"Is that why you do what you do?" Manu's voice was gentle, his thumb still moving in lazy circles, keeping her grounded as the memories flowed. "Giving people families?"

"Yeah," she replied softly. "Tons of people can have babies. Not everyone wants them. And a lot of people who want them can't have them. It's important to me that I know that the embryos I create are going to families who actively want their children. Patients are all screened for mental health issues, too, so I like to think that the work we do at North Hope Fertility means we're creating happy, healthy families. The kind of family I wish I could have had growing up."

"What about you? Do you want your own kids?"

She sighed, snuggling into his side, exhaustion from the

booze and crying jag weighing her down. Fatigue that let the truth slip from her lips. "No. I used to think I did. I would lie in bed and dream of having a child who knew they were the centre of my world. But the older I get, the more I think that's unrealistic. And I can't stand the thought of disappointing someone else." She grasped his hand and ran his fingers over her upper arm. Through the thin black wool of her sweater he would be able to feel the ridge, hard and straight, of her contraceptive implant. She could sense the sad smile creeping over her face. "No babies for me."

"Those things aren't permanent though, are they?" He brushed his hand over the silky black sheet of her hair.

She gave a small shrug. "They might as well be. It's my third."

"Permanent things scare me." His voice was quiet and she luxuriated in his fear being spoken out loud, the sense of safety in the bubble they'd created, even temporarily. "I sign short-term contracts, short-term leases. Nothing lasts forever. Nothing. Pretending otherwise is foolishness. Hoping for it is madness. Avali is the one permanent in my life and even then I feel the weight of it around my neck like a chain."

"Why is that?" She could hear the slur in her own voice as she pressed her face to his chest and inhaled the delicious clean scent of him.

"The pressure. All those people waiting to see what I'll do, waiting to tear me down if I make a wrong move."

"Like in league?"

"League is a game. It doesn't have the same impact. People's lives aren't ruined if I fumble the ball or lose a game." He paused. "I don't know how Aleki does it. Just the thought of that kind of responsibility puts the fear of the gods in me. The decisions he makes can change people's lives forever."

Her eyes fell shut, the darkness drowning out the last vestiges of light from the television.

That's silly. He'd be so good at it. I should tell him that.

"Well for what it's worth," she mumbled as sleep dragged her down. "I bet you'd be great at forever."

TEN

Clare's heels clicked across the marble lobby of the events centre and she tried not to wince at the noise. Usually she loved the click-clack of her scarlet fuck-me-or-fuck-off stilettos, but her nerves frayed at the thought of drawing undue attention to herself tonight. The annual North Hope Fertility Centre fundraiser was attended by all the board members, and despite the positive feedback Trish had given her regarding her recent work with the infertile cancer patient, her chest tightened at the idea of auditioning for them for hours on end.

And there could be no doubt that this was an audition. The board would be considering each of Trish's potential replacements carefully throughout the evening. Her small-talk game was about to be tested in the big leagues. Having Manu by her side tonight might have softened the sharp edge of anxiety, but he had his own charity auction event with the Knights at a nearby hotel. She'd come about as close as she got to begging him to blow it off and come with her instead, but he'd made it clear that attending was part of his job. More than that, he'd made it clear that he believed in her ability to do this alone.

God, I hope I don't let him down.

Outside the large windows, the setting sun shone golden across the waters of the Viaduct Basin, gleaming off the hulls of yachts and pleasure boats. The light was enough to give anyone a migraine. Clare squinted against nature's glory and hustled across the lobby fast enough that her shoes now resembled the percussion for a heavy metal concert. Finally, she reached carpet and breathed a small sigh of relief at being able to make her approach to the room the fundraiser was being held in without announcement.

The space was gorgeous, decorated with white flowers that were part of North Hope's branding. Silverware gleamed and glassware shone as she moved gratefully between the linen-draped tables towards the bar. As a good portion of attendees were current and former clients on alcohol cleanses, there was always miles too much booze at these things. She swiftly ordered a vodka tonic then turned to survey the room.

Take stock when you first arrive. Manu's instructions rang in her head. *There will be people who look out of place. Find those ones first. Those are your safety net. They'll be so grateful to have someone to talk to they won't mind if you're not the greatest conversationalist.*

She let her eyes scan over the crowd. The board bigwigs were there naturally, all jovial and red-faced with glasses of champagne their patients would kill for after years of sobriety. Former patients, some she recognised, in fancy dresses and nice suits, out for a night on the town away from their kids - those who North Hope hadn't provided with successful results rarely attended. And the staff, shiny and fresh, looking miles away from the scrubs and lab coats, the cold coffees and late nights and broken hearts and jubilation that went hand-in-hand with their jobs and kept people in the business of belief.

James was circling the room like a shark, all big teeth and flat eyes. Clare gratefully accepted her drink from the bar staff and swallowed her bitterness with a Russian chaser. She'd rather have a kidney stone than James's personality, but a part of her wished for his confidence in a crowd.

"Hi, Clare."

Clare turned. Hilary had appeared at the bar beside her as unobtrusively as Hilary did everything. The other team leader was about as memorable as a church mouse. She did her work quietly, ran her team quietly and went quietly home on time to a place where Clare could only assume she engaged in a number of soundless activities. Needlepoint, perhaps. Or maybe mime.

"Are you enjoying yourself?"

"Not really," Clare answered honestly.

Hilary grinned then, a huge one that cracked across her face and made her look like a completely different person.

"Me either," she confided, leaning closer, the swing of her light brown hair almost brushing Clare's shoulder. "I hate these things. But I love the chance to dress like a normal person and get away from my kid for the night, so it's a bit of a Catch-22."

Surprise tugged Clare's eyebrows higher on her forehead. *Hilary has a kid?* Hilary had already been at North Hope when Clare started working there. Suddenly the departures right at five o'clock made a bit more sense.

"Of course," she offered, nodding smoothly. She hoped it was smooth, anyway. "And how old is, um, your child now?"

Hilary smiled again. "Grace is nine." She whipped out a cell phone from somewhere and flashed it at Clare, who caught a glance of a toothy child with blonde pigtails and freckles.

"Cute," she acknowledged, taking another sip of her drink. Manu's voice echoed in her mind. *Keep the conversation going. Ask about the other person's interests.*

"Does she do needlepoint?"

Hilary flashed her a startled glance and laughed. "Grace? No, she does motocross "

Clare started. "With the motorbikes and the jumps and stuff?"

"Yeah," Hilary sighed, but there was an edge of pride to it. "Her dad got her into it and now she's obsessed. I spend half my life in muddy paddocks hoping she comes out unscathed. That's part of the reason I could use the lab manager promotion. My dad always said anything with tits or tyres was going to cost him money and I've got both."

Clare stared at Hilary as the other woman took a sip of wine, her own hand clutched around the frosty outside of her glass as Hilary's words swirled around in her head.

"You're applying for the lab manager position?" The words came out as a croak and she swallowed quickly, trying to push down the bubble of panic rising in her throat. James applying had been expected, Jeremy applying had been a concern, but Clare had never even considered that Hilary would throw her hat in the ring. Her mind whirred, trying to recall Hilary's statistics, the conferences she'd attended and articles she'd authored. Not a single thing came to mind. And that, right there, was the trouble with not making an effort to get along with her workmates. Now she was blindsided and had no idea of her competition's strengths.

Beside her, Hilary shrugged. "It'll be a shame to lose Trish, but I think I could do well in the role."

"Sure," Clare replied faintly. "Excuse me, please." She abandoned her glass on the bar and made her way towards the bathroom as quickly as she could in heels that were most definitely built for fashion over fleeing.

Shutting herself in a stall, she plonked down on the closed lid.

Stupid, stupid, stupid. The word echoed in her head, berating her for her arrogance. Of course Hilary would consider the position - for all the reasons Clare had, and probably more considering her motherhood revelation. Sitting up straight, she drew a deep breath into her diaphragm, held it for three, and released. Fuck, she wished Manu was here to talk her down. That man could see the bright side of a black hole.

Never mind, she told herself firmly. *You still have the best stats, the best results. So now you just need to beat out two people instead of one. You can do that.*

Equilibrium somewhat restored, she exited the bathroom, only to find James leaning against the wall of the corridor outside.

Ugh.

Clare went to move around him, but he spoke.

"Having a good night?"

Meeting his eyes reluctantly, she pasted on her best fake smile. "Of course. It's lovely to have the opportunity to raise money for the centre. And to see everyone outside of the lab," she tacked on quickly. A statement Manu had made her practice several times before she could leave the house to make her seem like a sociable potential lab manager instead of the angry hermit she was.

"Yes." James made a show of examining his nails, but his

casual stance wasn't fooling either of them. "Nice to make new acquaintances too, of course. Bet you're doing well in that area. You're such a peach when people get to know you." He smirked at her as she absorbed the blows, determined not to let him see her falter. The words swam in her head though, rustling up the insecurities she'd worked so hard to shove down.

"Have you had a chance to meet my date yet?" He didn't wait for her reply. "Yasmin Kircher. Lovely girl." He almost purred the last words, and Clare was trying so hard not to be sick in her mouth that the name took a moment to register.

"Yasmin Kircher. Any relation to Bob Kircher?" Her voice was clear, which was a miracle because *of course* she fucking was. Of course James was dating the fucking daughter of the Board chair at the exact moment he was up for a promotion.

His smirk grew wider, deeper. "Funnily enough, I think she might be. Families, eh? Can't pick 'em. But don't worry, Clare. I won't forget you when I'm at the top." Clapping a hand against her shoulder, he moved on down the hall towards the men's room and left Clare a seething ball of anger in black silk.

She strode down the hall, smacked the door to the ballroom open with one hand, walked directly to the bar where Hilary was talking with a tall, blonde woman and downed the drink she'd left there. At least, she hoped it was the drink she'd left there. It was a vodka and tonic, anyway, so she plunked the empty glass on the bar and gave the bartender the universal chin tilt for 'another'. While she waited, she turned back to the other women, the new one eyeing her nervously.

"Are you okay?" Hilary asked.

"Just stressed," she mumbled.

"Would you like some lavender oil to dab behind your ears?" Hilary asked. "I have some in my purse."

Jesus, she was nice. Clare felt even worse. James was fucking them both over, but at least she knew about it. At least she didn't have to go home and check on her nine-year-old and know the little girl's future was at the mercy of adult sexual politics.

"No, thanks." She drained the second vodka that arrived at her elbow and attempted a smile. "I, um, I actually need to talk to you about something. Can you excuse us for a minute, please?" She sent her customer service smile towards the other woman as she dragged Hilary a few feet down the bar. Any chance to practice.

"Oh my gosh, Clare. That was really rude." Hilary's eyes were wide.

"Hilary," she admonished. "It's important. I just bumped into James outside the bathroom. He's going to get the promotion."

Hilary looked shocked. "How can you possibly know that?"

"He just told me. He's dating Bob Kircher's daughter."

"That doesn't mean anything."

She pinched the bridge of her nose. "Hilary, I have the social tendencies of a mole, and even I know what the implications of that are. She'll tell her daddy how great James is at his job, daddy and James will play a round of golf or some such shite, and boom, the white man mafia strikes again. You and I will be team leaders until Grace is in her forties."

"Did he say that he was going to ask for special treatment?"

"He didn't have to."

A new voice joined the conversation. "What *did* he say?"

Surprised, Clare looked towards the tall woman, who had drifted back over to them. The blonde shrugged. "I couldn't help overhearing. I like workplace politics."

Clare rolled her eyes. "He told me he was dating her. Then he patted me on the shoulder like a five-year-old and told me he'll remember me when he's at the top."

"Interesting." The other woman tapped a finger against her lips. "That does sound like he plans to use her for her connections."

"Right?" Clare turned back to Hilary triumphantly. "See?"

"The question is whether he'll be successful though." The blonde woman mused. "I doubt it. Surely the woman in question knows how to keep business separate from pleasure."

Clare snorted. "No offence, but this is my career. I'd rather have a better strategy than hoping some rich daddy's girl can keep her brain out of her knickers. Have you met James? He'd chuck his nana under a bus to get ahead."

"I haven't even met you. How do I know you're not just trying to bury his chances for no reason?"

Clare examined this statement, saw the logic, and nodded in acknowledgement. "A fair point. I'm Clare Trescott, and I'm a team leader at North Hope."

"Nice to meet you, Clare." The blonde woman extended her hand and they shook. "I'm Yasmin Kircher."

MANU APPLAUDED POLITELY as the auctioneer slammed his hammer down and a luxury night boat ride through one of New Zealand's famous glow worm caves was sold to an Auckland real estate mogul. The prickle of discomfort under his skin shifted, nicking the centre of his chest as he imagined floating in the dark under a glittering roof with Clare by his side. Ever since their mutual masty session on the phone, images of the two of them together had been flashing through his mind.

He wanted to be with her. That much was clear. He was starting to crave her with the same fierce intensity he craved the championship or white bread during the season. He was gone for her. He had been since she first came around his fingers. And his need had only grown stronger since then, resulting in unexpected erections, long showers and one deeply undignified moment where he'd sniffed her coat just to get a hit of her warm lemon scent. He'd wanted to tell her this evening as he coached her through her bedroom door to settle her nerves about the fundraiser, but then she'd emerged wrapped in black silk and red leather and he'd lost the ability to vocalise.

It wouldn't be easy, he could acknowledge that. But plenty of players maintained long-distance relationships. Usually with people who'd indicated a slight interest in them outside of orgasms, but Manu refused to be deterred by that small detail.

A frosty bottle of beer appeared in front of him and he broke out of his reverie to see Finn plonk down in the next seat.

"Whatcha thinking about so hard over here?" The full-back took a pull of his own beer, his voice pitched low beneath the staccato of the auction noise.

"Nothing much." Manu slid his bottle back over towards Chalmers. He never drank more than two beers in public, and those had gone down much earlier in the evening with the image of Clare's cleavage in that dress stamped firmly in his mind.

"Bullshit." Chalmers laughed softly. "You're glaring at that centrepiece like it insulted your mama. Nobody looks like that at a fundraiser for kids with cancer unless they've got something on their mind."

Manu looked around, but nobody seemed to be paying attention to them. Most of the people he'd been seated with had drifted away after dinner, except for Hollis, who was slumped on the other side of the table sinking beers like they were the Titanic.

"It's Clare."

Finn nodded and clapped Manu on the shoulder. "I get it, man. Look, as someone who's an expert on waiting too long" - a shadow passed over the other man's face - "I say go for it. You regret a hundred percent of the shots you don't take, right?"

Manu nodded a tight-lipped confirmation, already liberating his phone from the confines of his suit pocket. Chalmers was right. Decisive action was the play of the day. He thumbed open his messaging app, vaguely aware of Hollis stumbling away from the table and a woman with a press badge taking the seat next to Chalmers.

Hey.

A scintillating start.

I like you. And I know you said we should just be flatmates but I want more. I want to wake up with you in the mornings and go out to the pub with you on Tuesdays. I want to be the rake to your governess. Just thought you should know.

Exhaling out the bubble of panic in his chest, Manu pressed the send button. He couldn't hear the *whoosh* as his feelings flew through space towards Clare, but the delivery icon popped up. Heat flushed over his body, and the collar of his shirt suddenly felt too tight. He sat in discomfort, panic flaring through his body until the auction ended. As soon as the gavel slammed down on the final item, Manu loosened his tie and undid the first two buttons of his shirt as he stood and headed towards the hotel entrance for some air.

He got as far as the lobby.

Hollis was there, wrapped around some girl. Manu was halfway past them before the details sank into his brain, connecting slowly like awkward-fitting jigsaw pieces.

Black hair. Black silk. Pale curves. Red shoes. *Clare*.

He spun on his heel and stalked towards them. Gaining ground, he could see that Hollis was in full flirt mode, while Clare leaned slightly away from him, more focused on her phone - *holy shit, her phone* - than on the Knights' captain's attempts to share his venereal diseases with her.

"Clare." His voice rang out in the high-ceilinged space. She turned towards him, but his gaze was still focused on fucking Hollis and his smug smile. "You alright?"

"No. It was a disaster." At that, he pulled his gaze from Hollis and examined Clare. Smudges of dark makeup pooled under her lower lashes, her lipstick was gone, possibly due to the way she was worrying her bottom lip with her teeth, and her shoulders were bowed. She looked defeated.

He was by her side in a flash, reaching for her hand. "What happened?"

"I fucked it all up." Her huge grey eyes rose to meet his. "I insulted the daughter of the Board chair. I'll be lucky if I have a job on Monday, let alone a shot at the promotion."

"They can't fire you for that!"

"Maybe not. But they can make it uncomfortable for

me." Her gaze travelled over his face, lingering on his lips. "I was already on my way over here when I got your text."

Hope, mingling with nerves, sparked in his chest. She'd already been coming to him. His throat worked as he waited for a sign, anything that told him he hadn't overstepped, that she felt the same.

"Ah, I wouldn't worry about your job, babe." Hollis's voice filtered through the taut air between them. "Esera here can support you. Well, for the next month or so until he fucks off overseas for good and abandons us all."

Manu's tentative hope wavered as Clare pulled back slightly, her gaze darting to Hollis. "What do you mean?"

Hollis guffawed. "He hasn't told you? He's only in Auckland until the season finishes. Then he'll be traded back to an Aussie team. Thinks he's too good for all of us here."

"Is that true?" Clare's eyes searched Manu's like she could read his mind. Shame and anger curdled in his gut, hot and sour.

"Yes." No point denying it. He had no idea how Hollis had gotten hold of that information, but it was a conversation he'd been planning to have with her soon.

"You're leaving?" Clare's voice was high, incredulous. "You sent me that text knowing you'd be leaving in the next few weeks?"

"It's not like that." They were gaining some attention now, other guests and a few members of the press who'd been present for the charity event. Manu didn't think they were close enough to overhear, but he lowered his voice regardless. "I was going to tell you. I needed to know how you felt about me first. If there was something here worth investigating further."

"Something worth investigating?" She echoed the words

slowly, her controlled tone totally at odds with the pain in her eyes that cut him to the quick. "I'm not a second-hand car, Manu. I hardly need an inspection if you're just looking for a stopover shag."

Frustration leaked out in his voice. "It's more than sex, Clare. Though, yes, that is something I would like to do with you." He moved, angling his body between her and Hollis, placing his hand on her elbow and dropping his voice an octave. "Is that something you'd like to do with me?"

A shiver ran through her under his palm. Gods, she was sweet. He was dying for a taste.

"Yes." Her response was almost a whisper, but from the way his body reacted below the belt she might as well have been shouting her intent from the rooftops. All the blood in his body shot south, leaving him lightheaded.

"Besides," she breathed, "you're only here for a little while. We might as well make the most of it."

Discomfort stirred in his belly at the reminder. "You're okay with that?"

The sweetness of her smile caught him off guard. "I like you too, Manu. But there's no point worrying about things we can't change. You're leaving. And I can think of a *lot* of things I'd like to do with you before you go." Her finger trailed down the buttons of his shirt.

A caustic laugh razed over them, penetrating the fantasy that they were alone. "That's cute. Let me know when you're done with her, yeah? I can wait a few weeks for a girl like this."

Manu spun, anger sparking in his blood, but Clare moved like a streak of dark lightning around him, impossibly fast. Hidden from the crowd by the volume of her skirt, her hand went straight to Hollis's crotch and twisted,.

The sound of breaking glass echoed in the space as Hollis's beer bottle slid to the marble floor. It competed with the clicks of media cameras, but Clare showed no sign of hearing any of it as she tipped her jaw up so that her lips were near Hollis's ear. Manu was just close enough to hear the low threat that passed between them.

"You talk about me like that again, I'll break your dick off. Do you understand me?"

Hollis's head bobbed, his throat working fast. "Yes."

Clare released him and stood back. Hollis fell into the chair he'd been in when Manu arrived, breathing heavily, his angry eyes fixed on Clare. She turned on her heel and strode for the exit, one hand reaching out to tow Manu along behind her. He wanted to cheer, but the click of cameras and her heels and the rush of pride and lust in his ears was deafening as it was.

"What now?" Manu asked, once they were safely outside in the low light of the city street, his adrenal rush fading now that the lights, cameras and Hollis were behind them. There would be fallout, no doubt, but that was a thought for later, not now, when Clare's soft hand was pressed against his and her perfume mingled with the crisp midnight scent of the City of Sails.

"Now?" Clare asked, looking up at him with luminous eyes, and he fell headfirst into her liquid gaze. She smiled, slow and sure, and his dick tightened behind his zip. She rose up on her toes, her breath hot against his neck, and placed the gentlest of kisses on the corner of his mouth. Manu almost came in his pants. "Now I think we should go home."

ELEVEN

They rode home in silence, each looking out the windows of their Uber, linked only by their hands in the middle of the backseat and the anticipation that built itself into a bonfire between them. Heat snapped at Clare every time Manu dragged a calloused thumb across the inside of her wrist, the temperature rising with each kilometre closer to home they travelled.

By the time they reached the apartment building, she was ready to combust. She slid across the seat and followed him out of the car, still clutching at him as if he might just disappear, like a figment of her horny imagination, leaving her lusty and alone.

She needn't have worried. As soon as they were in the apartment and the door had shut behind them with a soft snick, Manu turned towards her, shifting his hands to her hips. He lowered his head to hers, pressing their temples together, and awareness skittered through her with an accompanying shiver.

"Second thoughts?" His voice was low and ripe with need.

Her pulse jumped. "No."

"Good."

His jaw scraped a path up her neck in response, trailing fire, and she forgot how to breathe. Shuddering with white-hot desire, she tucked her chin for fear that any additional stimulation would set her screaming away from the dark promise of pleasure.

"Uh-uh, sweetheart." Manu tipped her chin up. "Show me that pretty face." He tipped her chin up, his gaze boring into hers. "That's it." Bending his head, he gently tugged at her bottom lip with his teeth. "Fuck, I love this mouth. I've been dreaming of it for weeks."

Clare snaked her tongue out to flick his top lip and he growled, biting her lip softly before releasing it. "Are you going to let me have your mouth tonight?"

"Yes." Need threaded through her voice but she didn't give a fuck. She'd been avoiding these feelings for weeks and all she'd felt was hollow and sick. Now that Manu was here with her, running his big hands down her sides, ruffling her hair with his breath and setting her nerve endings alight, he could have whatever he wanted.

Manu cursed softly, the filthy word brushing against the shell of her ear as he buried his face in her neck and sucked.

"No hickeys," she gasped out, hanging on to the final straw of self-preservation she had left. Or perhaps just a Pavlovian response from her teen years. He raised his head, flames lighting his gaze.

"I've been waiting for you for weeks that feel like years, lo'u alofa. Finally, you are mine. If you don't want a sign of that on your neck, I can respect that. But make no mistake, I will mark you tonight."

"Guh," Clare responded eloquently, as heat flooded her core.

"Would you like to move to the bedroom?" Manu tucked a swath of hair behind her ear. "It might give me more opportunity to examine my canvas." He snapped his teeth at her, a jokey kind of amusement lifting one side of his mouth, but his eyes remained hungry.

"We could go to the bedroom," Clare offered. "But, Manu, are you sure about—"

"Stop asking me if I am sure, Clare. I'm not a virgin. I'm a grown man, and I have made up my mind."

"Okay," she replied meekly. "I've made up my mind too."

"About what, sweetheart?" Manu reached around to palm her arse and she went up on the balls of her feet, pressing against his erection.

So good.

She nipped at his jaw. "I was going to go easy on you, given your lack of recent experience, but I've changed my mind." Lowering her voice to a whisper she stretched higher on her toes. "I'm gonna suck you so hard, you black out."

At the stunned look on his face, she bounced back out of his arms and took off towards the hallway. "Catch me if you can!"

Delight split her face in half as she heard him crash into something behind her, his profanity painting the air blue. She hit her bedroom at full force, twisting the knob as she shouldered the door open, and then she flew across the room towards the bed. She was almost there when a solid wall of muscle lifted her, tossed her and followed her down, one thick thigh resting between her knees as she giggled - *giggled* - into the blankets she was now face down on.

"If you are trying to gain the upper hand," Manu murmured, palming the exposed globe of her arse where her dress had ridden up, "there is no need. You've always had it."

The delicious press of him at her back lifted, and the fabric of her dress moved up to her waist on both sides as he skimmed his palms up the outside of her thighs.

"Is this for me?" He tugged at her thong, pulling the fabric tight over her mound, and she squirmed as it just missed her clit.

"For you," she gasped.

"What a precious gift." He moved then, pressing her thighs further apart to accommodate himself and shifting her underwear to the side. "I know just how to say thank you."

The first touch of his tongue to her folds shot electricity through her. Hitching her hips up, Manu fell on her like a ravenous man. He licked at her, his broad tongue eagerly lapping up the never-ending evidence of her desire as she pressed her face to the mattress and rocked back towards him, seeking more of his mouth. His growl vibrated against her and she shivered. Then he was moving, turning behind her, the silk of his hair sliding against her inner thighs as he worked himself into position on his back and wove his strong arms around the tops of her legs to pull her down onto his mouth.

His enthusiasm was still there, but now so was finesse, as he ate at her with slow, devastating precision. His tongue stroked higher, sweeping over her clit once, twice, three times, and she whimpered, the needy sound cutting through the rough pants that rose from their combined bodies and filled the air above them. She felt him smile, the wicked curve of his lips playing over her sensitive folds. Then he lifted her slightly and his voice drifted up to her. "Do you like that, lo'u alofa?"

Moaning, she pushed her hips back and down, frantically seeking his mouth, and his chuckle brushed against her clit like a tease as he banded his arms more firmly around her and pressed her onto the generous flat of his tongue. He kept licking up, up, up, his lips fixing around the sensitive bud and suckling. The pull of desire radiated through her, from her nipples down through her stomach to the place where his lips met flesh, twisting in a heady buzz of greedy lust as she pressed down against him, seeking more, more, more.

Despite her hunger, he kept up an almost leisurely pace. Soft, hot, sucking kisses at her clit as he kneaded the flesh of her thighs and held her to his mouth as the pressure rose, dizzyingly hot, prickling at her skin and twisting until she shattered. Brightly, brilliantly and completely, a screaming mess.

He kept up the sweet assault as she came down, the oblivion fading as reality seeped back in, the dark of the room, the cool cotton of the bedsheet against her cheek and the languorous blanket of bliss that settled over her. She barely noticed as he slid out from under her, a strong hand stroking down her back and smoothing over her hip, until his gorgeous, accented voice murmured in her ear.

"You didn't think we were done, did you lo'u alofa?"

MANU EASED Clare's thong down her hips, the dampness of the red lace akin to the roar of a home crowd.

Me. I did that.

Pride thundered in his chest as he worked her underwear off, dropped them on the floor and slid his hands up the length of her legs. She wasn't a small woman, but his hands looked huge on her, dark brown and calloused against the creamy softness of her thighs.

The curve of her arse was a miracle, and he bent his head to bite and lick it, before trailing a parade of kisses up her spine. She shivered, and he sucked gently at the spot where her shoulder met her neck.

"Cold?"

"No."

He smiled against her skin. "I should hope not." He lowered himself slowly, keeping his upper body and core engaged so that his front merely brushed against her back. She moaned, the sound wrapping around his dick like a fist, as she arched her back and pressed the lush swell of her behind against him.

For a second, Manu lost the ability to see. When his vision returned and she was still there, pushing that gift of flesh against his aching length in hot little pulses, sensation drove him to shift his weight down and forward to bury his cock between her cheeks and rock his hips forward to meet her.

They ground against each other for long, delicious moments, the evidence of Clare's earlier orgasm smoothing the process. He leant forward and nuzzled his nose into her hair as he glided back and forth between the full globes of her backside. Inhaling deeply, the scent of lemons took him to the edge as effectively as the tiny whimpers she made as she wriggled her soft body back and forth underneath him.

"Is this what you wanted, lo'u alofa? Or did you think that I would be so eager to be inside this beautiful body that I would lose my head and spill all over you the first time you touched me?"

"No. Maybe. I don't know. *More*."

He tilted his hips and dragged the head of his cock

across the silken crease of her lips, the filthy kiss of her mois-
ture on his tip enough to make his eyes roll back in his head.

Fighting not to prove them both right, he pulled back,
the cool air doing nothing to alleviate the fire in his balls as
he ran a hand down the pale length of her back.

"Turn over, love. I want to see you the first time."

She hesitated, he saw it in the tensing of her shoulders,
but she acquiesced. Triumph bore through him as he rolled
the condom on and fisted himself. He watched her settle
back, her black hair spilling like a tangled crown across the
covers, grey eyes wide and wild with want.

He ducked his head and licked her, a wet stripe over her
stomach and up her sternum, claiming her lips with his at
the end.

Lifting his mouth from hers, he sought her eyes. "Put
me in, Clare."

She rushed to obey, her hand hot and greedy against his
erection as she guided him to her entrance. And then he
was inside, gliding deep, every nerve ending on fire as he
slid into place between her soft thighs.

His voice echoed in the air around them, curses, gratitude and prayers mingling together in Avalian and English
as she pulled her knees back so the base of his cock bumped
against her centre. Then she stretched up and nipped at his
bottom lip, the sharp little bite cutting through the cloud of
sensation fogging his brain.

"Come on then, superstar." She grinned up at him, her
features imprinting themselves on his brain. "Show me
what you got."

He moved then, a quick thrust in and out, her gasp like
music to his ears, and he repeated it, again and again, one
foot braced on the mattress as he drove forward into her
body, pulling back slowly then snapping his hips forward,

curling one hand under her thigh so he could hold her open.

Clare cried out, grasping at his arse as though he could get further inside her, as though each pump into her didn't have his balls slapping her skin, as if the tip of him wasn't buried as deep into paradise as he could get.

"Fuck, Manu," his little wildcat gasped, and the sound of his name on her lips as he ground into her almost undid him completely.

"How do you want it, baby?" Desire was pulling at his balls in an iron grip, but he refused to give in.

Not before her. Not before her.

The words became a chant in his mind, setting the rhythm of his thrusts, and he prayed to the gods he could last through her climax before erupting like the Mount Vesuvius of boning.

"Me on top."

Clare tilted her hips forward even as she spoke, and he followed her lead, eating up the little gasps she made with kisses. Three more pumps and he rolled, holding her tight to him so that, when the world came right again, she was straddling him, gravity aiding the sweet press of her down onto his lap. She tightened around him immediately, and he raised his upper body, one thumb seeking the hard little nub of her clit. He pressed it gently, not rubbing, just letting Clare work herself on his hand and his dick, her movements growing frenzied.

"More." Her voice was high, need threaded through it. "Harder."

Manu surged up further, his mouth claiming her nipple. He latched his teeth onto the bud; not hard, just enough to scrape against the tender flesh as they moved. He pumped up once, twice, three times, deep and fast.

Clare went off like a bomb. She stopped moving and her internal walls locked around him like a vice, claiming him as she spewed heat over the thick column of his erection and down.

"Fuck, that's it." His voice was a gasp. "Soak my lap, baby." He pounded up into her, lost to everything except the wild slick slide, the scent of lemons and arousal, and the tremor of her body as she slowly unclenched around him and slumped forward, soft and sated, as his balls tightened and electricity crackled under his skin.

Clutching Clare's chin, he angled her head and kissed her, sloppy and unpracticed, before pulling back from her mouth and roaring his release into the dark.

TWELVE

Clare hummed on her way into work on Monday. It was obnoxious, but she didn't care. If she'd known what the stamina of professional athletes was like, she'd have thrown herself at Manu the instant he walked in the door. They could have been banging like bunnies for a month now. Though, she reasoned, it was unlikely her body could have handled such an intense workout for so long. Probably better to only have a couple of weeks of it, lest her muscles give out from overuse. A Saturday morning yoga class once every few months hadn't quite prepared her for the flexibility her new hobby required. The thought, and the corresponding tenderness in her thighs, made her smile.

Lying in bed this morning, she and Manu had compared schedules - her on her phone's calendar app, and him from memory. There was their fake - *was it still fake?* - date on Tuesday, and Manu was leaving Friday morning for a game over in Australia on Saturday night. When she'd shown him her colour-coded workflow chart that kept her at work until after seven most weeknights, he'd taken her phone from her hands and typed 'Sexy Times with Manu' in red boxes beginning at 5.30pm each day. It was a mark of how much she liked him that his thumbs remained intact after touching her calendar. In fact, she'd found it delightful.

Her good mood buoyed her all through the morning. She bopped away happily to the music in her wireless earbuds as she worked through the stack of paperwork on her desk, the grunt work she despised but spent sixty percent of her time doing because leadership roles paid the bills better than lab work ever could. She'd just switched over to her 'Basic Bitch Club Bangers' playlist and settled down to eat her lunchtime salad (for her health) and donut (for her soul) when a cell phone landed on her desk next to her jumbo reusable coffee cup.

Yanking an earbud out, she glanced up at Jeremy. "What's this?"

"Article on The Waka's site you should see," he replied, rolling a spare chair over and unwrapping a sub the length of her arm. Biting into it, he watched her scroll down the news page, nodding when she stopped abruptly.

"There it is."

He fished a bar of chocolate out of his pocket and extended it to her, but she ignored it, dismay filling her stomach as she took in the pictures. She and Matt Hollis sitting on the chairs in the lobby with him leaning towards her. Manu standing between them and looking at her with heat in his eyes. Her and Hollis, her face tilted up as she whispered an unheard threat in his ear, with the bottle smashed to smithereens beside them. Her and Manu holding hands on the way out of the hotel. Another shot, blurrier, of Manu holding the Uber door open as she climbed in, the black silk of her skirt hitched up to reveal a significant amount of leg highlighted by the glow of a streetlight.

Knights Battle Over More Than A Championship the headline screamed, and she skimmed the article, the analytical side of her brain cataloguing the pertinent data. She was a slut, leading them on, driving a wedge between teammates, poor Matt Hollis's wife ... Every ridiculous stereotype about women and sports players and interpersonal relationships laid out in black and white on a national news site. And there, at the bottom of the page, a screenshot of her LinkedIn profile. A decent photo - her dark hair was brushed and styled, her smile almost believable - right above the words 'Team Leader at North Hope Fertility Centre.'

Her heart sank. Oh no. No, no, no. Not her workplace. She couldn't have North Hope dragged into this. The clinic prided itself on discretion. People came from all over the country for North Hope's services, famous people even. Well, New Zealand famous. If reporters began camping outside the clinic hoping for a shot of her, she could kiss the promotion goodbye. As if she hadn't fucked things up enough with Yasmin Kircher.

Over the rushing in her ears, she could still hear the music, T.I. tinnily reminding her that she could have whatever she liked. *Not fucking likely, mate.* Not anymore. Jesus, when had her life become so complicated? All she'd ever wanted was a stable life - a decent place to live, a job that allowed her financial security and the ability to help others. Maybe a cat one day. Then Manu Esera had swanned into her life, all big shoulders and bigger heart, sexy enough to stop traffic, and turned it upside down.

"Oh my God, there you are," Hilary breathed, dropping into another chair. "Is it true you're banging a patient?

That's the stupidest idea I've ever heard. Do you *want* James to win?"

Bitterly, Clare remembered back forty-eight hours when Hilary had been too nervous to maintain eye contact with her for more than a heartbeat. Then the words struck home, each one laced with career-ending poison.

"What?" The word was dragged from her.

She looked frantically to Jeremy, who pressed his lips together and raised an eyebrow in sympathetic acknowledgement. Spinning to face her computer, she pulled up the internal patient database and typed 'Hollis' in. The results were up in a fraction of a second. Matthew Herd Hollis and Lauren Pamela Hollis. They were working with James's team, but that meant nothing. A North Hope patient was a North Hope patient and they were - rightly - off limits. It didn't matter that she hadn't done anything. Didn't matter that she'd been threatening him in the shot the site claimed showed 'an intense sexual connection'. In fact, threatening a man's testicles would likely be even worse for her chances at retaining employment if the truth came out.

"Clare," Trish barked, striding into the open-plan office area, James trailing behind her in a cloud of vengeful triumph. "My office. Now."

Clare's stomach twisted, the familiar clench of apprehension tightening under her ribs. Slowly, she stood and followed Trish down the hall where the management offices peeled off on either side. She closed the door quietly behind her and sat carefully on one white chair, eyes locked on her lap.

"Are you fucking Matt Hollis?" Trish's words were sharp but not unkind.

"No," Clare whispered, an icky, awful heat crawling over her body.

"Are you planning to?"

"No."

"Thank Christ for that," Trish sighed out. She rustled in her top drawer, pulled out a red box of Korean choco pies and tossed one at Clare, whose instincts in catching flying sweets in her peripheral vision were clearly unaffected by the shame that coated her body. She automatically took a bite, the yellow sponge and marshmallow under the choco-late coating melting in her mouth. *Yum.* She'd have to find out where to get these before Trish left. Or before she was fired.

"Look," Trish continued, swallowing her own bite of heaven, "you've always been a reliable employee. Solid. Stable. Sure, you could use some development in patient support, but everyone has their thing. This though? A scandal in the national news? With a patient, no less. And James is blathering on about you undermining him with the daughter of the board. I don't know what's going on, Clare, but it's not working in your favour right now."

The rebuke stung despite its soft delivery. Clare hunched her shoulders against the impact, curling tight around the hard knot in her stomach. This. This was why she worked longer hours than anyone, why she read more studies now than she had at university. This was why she didn't - couldn't - open herself up to anyone. Because this feeling of failure, of disappointing someone who might believe in her was too much to bear. Humiliation rose like a wave inside her, lapping at her nerves, sending hot little pinpricks dancing under her skin as she fought against the voices that echoed in her mind.

Not good enough. Not the right fit. Why can't you just be normal?

She swallowed them down, packing her insecurities

tightly into the suitcase in her mind so she could pull them out and examine them later. It was a habit that had served her well growing up. People didn't mind hurting you, but they didn't like to see evidence of it. It was too messy, went against the narrative of themselves as the heroes of their own stories. The most important thing now was to keep her shit together. Wavering in the face of this conversation would only serve to highlight her unsuitability for the promotion. If, by some small miracle, she was still even in the running. Breathing through her nose, she looked up, meeting Trish's dark gaze across the desk.

"I'm sorry for the media attention," Clare began slowly. "It is unfortunate, but I can assure you I am not romantically involved with Matt Hollis, nor will I ever be."

"And Manu Esera?" Trish watched her carefully.

"I am not romantically involved with him, either." Sex wasn't a romantic involvement, and she'd embrace celibacy before she put her career at risk for her vagina's desires. "What I am, what I have always been, is one hundred percent dedicated to this company and the work that we do. I cannot apologise for what has already happened, but I can assure you that nothing is more important to me than my job here helping to give our patients the families they dream of." She paused, steeling herself before vowing. "I will not let anything or anyone interfere with my ability to continue to do that."

***

"MANU! Manu, tell us about the fight!"

"What are things like between you and Matt Hollis now?"

Tension knotted between Manu's shoulder blades,

pulling them tighter as he windmilled his arms through the warmup sequence. Reporters had been crowding around the edges of the field since the team ran out for training fifteen minutes ago and so far he'd managed to avoid looking over once, even as the questions grew more audacious, skating the slippery line between journalism and gossip.

He clenched his jaw, bristling as the clicking of cameras increased in a frenzy. Hollis must have arrived. Sure enough, the slimy idiot approached from his left. He extended a hand to Manu, a jovial smile that didn't reach his eyes pasted onto his pale, bloated face. Grinding out a similar smile, Manu shook his hand. They both knew the score - this was for the cameras and the cameras only. The quarter-finals were next week, and Harro would shoot them both if they let a personal matter overshadow the media narrative of a team brought back from the brink.

"You better stay out of my way off the field." Hollis murmured from behind his bared teeth as they shook, longer and harder than necessary.

"How's your wife, dickhead?" Manu ground back.

Hollis narrowed his eyes and opened his mouth but a sharp whistle cut through the air before he could respond.

"Alright ladies, that's enough nattering. Let's get on with it."

"Coach, you gotta stop using language that equates femininity with weakness. That shit is messed up."

The entire team, trainers and all, stilled and stared at Rangi Katu. The rookie shrugged, as though he hadn't just thrown a verbal grenade into the middle of their training session. "Well it is. Women buy forty percent of our tickets."

Harro's face was an interesting shade of purple. Manu could practically see his internal struggle - forty years as a pro turned coach in a sport that upheld traditional masculinity as a banner versus the media storm of sexism in the sport if he responded badly right now in front of the cameras.

"Right," Harro croaked out eventually. "Well. Onto ball drills." He jerked his head towards Manu and Hollis. "You two. See me at the end of training."

They trudged over to the far side of the stadium an hour later, sweaty and red-faced. Harro set down his tablet and pierced them with an icy glare. His voice matched his eyes for arctic chill. "What the fuck was that on Saturday?" They were too far away for any of the media mics to pick up sound, and fortunately most of the journos had quietened down when it became apparent that training wasn't going to devolve into an MMA fight night.

Hollis shrugged sullenly and Manu stared at the ground.

Disbelief rolled off Harro in waves. "You're not going to talk about it?"

Silence.

"Well, hear this. If either one of you takes a piss without checking with me over the next two weeks, you won't see the inside of a changing shed again until you hit your forties. From this moment on, you are a Knight and a Knight only. Nothing personal matters. Not until this season wraps up. You can deal with all of your bullshit then, but now is the time to focus on the game. Esera, you're right where you wanted to be, but unless you can pull your bloody head in and work as part of this team on the field and off, I won't be shopping you anywhere. And you?" Disgust laced his tone as he turned his attention to Hollis. "You're the fucking captain, Hollis. But you're showing zero leadership. None of these boys want to follow you into battle. I should strip your captaincy for this week's game but that will just throw off the whole squad and keep these news buzzards hovering. But you're on thin ice, boy."

He paused. Manu met his coach's eyes dead on, which was a feat in itself since he felt about two inches bloody tall. He hadn't had a dressing down like this in years. Harro nodded curtly, dismissing them, and they trailed back towards the tunnel to the dressing rooms, ignoring the renewed questioning by the media still hanging around.

Manu showered and dressed in record time, thankful that the sheds had cleared out a bit. The players still left shot him looks out the corners of their eyes but nobody approached him. They would all have had their arses handed to them by Harro a time or two as well. Rugby league coaches were notorious for their short fuses.

His relief was just as short though. As soon as he exited the stadium into the parking lot, the reporters were on him - cameras popping, firing questions. They hadn't left at all, just changed positions so they could catch him alone.

Stupid. The thought ran through his head. He should have known better, should have thought to go out the back entrance, but he'd been a million miles away, with Harro and his threats and the plays for Saturday's game, and the desire to get home to Clare and unload about his day, cuddled into her soft curves on the couch.

One of the reporters bumped him, sending him stumbling to his knees, and that was all it took.

Pressure rose in his chest, closing his throat as the memories flashed in front of his eyes. One hand on the dashboard, hot under the power of the island sun. The impact of the cars, slamming him forward until the seatbelt jerked him backwards, his head bouncing off the window as agony screamed up his leg, hot and fiery, like nothing he'd ever felt in years of sports injuries. Then the noise. The screech of metal, the howl of sirens, people yelling and banging on the doors, trying to open them. And he turned, almost blinded by pain and deafened by the impact, to check on Tua.

Tua, who had a son at home and a wife who loved him. Tua, who had been his best friend since primary school. Who had never touched alcohol, a cigarette, drugs or supplements of any kind because he wanted to be the best, and the best player was one who lived and played clean he used to say. Tua, whose eyes were open, staring unseeing at Manu as blood dripped down his forehead where it rested on the steering wheel. Tua, who didn't move when Manu reached over to shake him, to plead and beg and scream for him to look at him, to turn his head, to sit up. Tua, who had wanted it all - *deserved it all* - and had his life cut short by the ruthless ambition of the gossip-mongering media jackals who circled the royal family, ruining them piece by piece. Just like they were ruining him now.

He closed his eyes against the deluge of memories, against the pain that rose in his chest like a tidal wave, against the sights and sounds that had put him back in that place, helpless and heartbroken while he waited for the ambulance personnel to arrive. And he heard it again, the gunning of an engine, but this time it stopped, this time it idled nearby and a voice rang out over the caws of the vultures who had come to pick over his bones.

"Let the lad have a bit of air, yeah? Stand back would ya?" Finn Chalmers, the golden boy of the game, coming to his rescue. The journalists scattered immediately. Prince Charming they'd dubbed him his first season, and it had stuck. Finn might as well walk on water for all the fans he had in the city newsrooms. He hooked one hand under Manu's elbow and helped him to his feet.

"Might not want to take the bus today, huh?" His voice was low, and Manu clung to it as the cloak of trauma slipped away and allowed him to focus on the now.

"Maybe not," he mumbled, and let himself be guided to Finn's car. Once they were on the road he concentrated on regulating his breathing.

"Home or mine?" Finn asked.

"Home's fine. Clare should be home early tonight." At least he hoped so. They had a shared sex entry on her calendar, but really he just wanted to see her, to breathe in her lemon-fresh scent and hear about her day at work and let her soothe him into forgetting.

Chalmers dropped him off outside the apartment building, making him promise to call if he needed anything. He headed upstairs and threw himself on his navy comforter to stare at the ceiling for a while. He only moved when the phone rang. Checking the caller ID, he answered in Avalian. *Talk about timing.*

"Good morning, troublemaker."

Kai's giggle echoed through the speaker. "Hi, Uncle."

"Shouldn't you be in school?" Tua's son was seven now and every bit the conscientious student his father had been.

"I'm leaving in a minute. But Mum said I could ring and ask you about your new girlfriend."

Manu groaned into the phone. "Where do you hear this nonsense?"

"In the papers." Avali's single newspaper still had a monopoly on the island's news, despite the other media sources that had grown with international advances in technology.

Kai's mother came on the line. "She looks pretty. When are you bringing her home to meet us all?"

"You're as bad as your son," Manu growled, his heart

warming as Tina laughed down the line. She hadn't laughed for a long time after Tua died. Neither had he.

"We're just kidding." His godson's mother paused. "It would be nice if it were true though. We want to see you happy. He would want you to be happy too."

"I know." He sighed. "And I will be happy. When I win the championship and hand Kai the medal his dad should have been able to give him."

"Alright," Tina replied softly. "But Kai knows how much Tua loved him. And he knows how much you love him too. He doesn't need a medal to be reminded of that."

"But I need to give it to him." It was the only way he could make amends to his buried friend.

"You do what you need to do, Manu. Are you coming home after the season?"

"Come home, Uncle!" Kai's voice crowed in the background and a soft laugh escaped Manu.

"I will. Kai can come stay with me for a week, give you a bit of a break."

They hung up shortly after, Kai's departing words some advice for Manu's defence against the Bulls in his upcoming game. He wandered out to the living room, watched a couple of movies and cooked dinner at seven, but Clare never appeared. He gave up waiting at ten and went to bed.

THIRTEEN

The whistle cut through the air like a knife.

"Esera, you bloody muppet! What are you doing?"

Manu slowed to a jog, his fingers tightening on the rough surface of the ball.

"The gap was there." Frustration leaked out in his voice.

"I don't give a fuck if there was a hole the size of the Panama canal in front of you. I told you to pick and go." Harro's flinty eyes sharpened on him. "These drills build teamwork and that's something you sorely need. You've only been here a hot minute."

He nodded tightly and handed the ball off to the half-back, who gave him a sympathetic look and ran it back to start the play again.

As he coasted through a dozen pick and go drills, his mind wandered back to Harro's words.

These drills build teamwork, and that's something you sorely need.

He'd never had trouble fitting into a team before, but a month into his contract with the Knights and he had yet to fully find his place. Finn was a joker but held a great deal of mana and respect with the men as a group, and Manu was grateful for his help in settling in. Victor Hewitt was the veteran, built like a skyscraper but always talking quietly with younger players, helping them with plays or personal issues. Rangi Katu, the good-looking rookie, was the trouble-maker, in and out of the papers, which the rest of the team plastered over his locker most Monday mornings. Matt Hollis was still an arsehole and therefore forgettable.

And then there was him - an import, an outsider, someone who by the rights of talent and skill should have been welcomed with open arms to a team in desperate need of both, but he wasn't quite sure he had been and the knowledge niggled at him like the sharp edge of a stone in his cleats.

The muggy Australian air wrapped around him, weighing him down. He'd played at the Bulls field in Sydney before, when he'd been with the Giants, but being here in unfamiliar colours and unsure of his role made him feel like a rookie all over again. Being a teammate was simply who he was - part of his identity. It had been since he and Tua had joined the under-eights as skinny little six-year-olds. Without it ... well, without it he was just a poor shadow of his brother.

The same brother who had called him just that morning and instructed him to get on the family's private plane to Avali as soon as he was finished with tonight's game. No further information, other than assuring Manu he would be back in New Zealand for his Monday morning training. Knowing Aleki, it could be anything from an impending natural disaster to a desire to play pool. His brother's therapist was all about family bonding time, but as much as Manu appreciated the opportunities to hone his table skills and see his future sister-in-law, the apprehension that he might somehow be dragged into a decision-making position in the kingdom set his teeth on edge.

He was already tense this week. After their glorious sex-a-thon the weekend before, Clare had seemed off, working late every night - even Tuesday, meaning she missed her standing booking at the pub. Perhaps he'd come on too strong. Between their bouts of adult activities and bad jokes, as they'd lain tangled in her sheets, he'd told her about Tua and the accident. About wanting to win a championship for him. It had felt right at the time, but maybe something about the story had triggered a bad reaction in her.

The thought niggled at him throughout the rest of the day, quietly stitching its way into thoughts it had no place in as he prepared for his most important game in months. Winning this game would clear the way for them to play in the quarter-finals next week. He'd be free from the Knights at the end of the season, free to pursue the championship he'd been working towards for years. The championship Tua should have claimed.

The first peal of the whistle cleared his past from his head as instinct took over and he dove into action, running, passing and tackling. After the game, buoyed by the hard-fought victory and the bone deep satisfaction of having played an absolute blinder, he checked his phone. The reward of seeing Clare's name in his notifications was equal to that of the scoreboard on the field outside their visitors' changing room.

Saw you won. Congratulations. Lasagne to celebrate tomorrow.

The memory of the last time he'd had lasagne hit him like a freight train and he closed his eyes and willed his body to behave, lest he become known as the guy who sported wood at the mention of Italian food. In his workplace.

His phone dinged again and he checked it eagerly.

Aleki. *A car is waiting outside to take you to the airstrip. See you soon.*

Manu cursed softly and navigated back to Clare's message. *Sorry,* he typed out. *Change of plans. I'm heading to Avali. I'll be home after training on Monday. Save me some lasagne?* After some deliberation over whether adding an emoji would make him look desperate, he thumbed a smiley face onto the end of the message and hit send before he could second-guess himself.

After a quick shower, his phone pinged again as he was getting dressed and hope soared in his chest.

Get in the car, dickhead.

He sent his brother the middle finger emoji in response, but despite his tight hold on his phone on the short drive from the Bulls stadium to the private airstrip, it remained quiet and he was forced to switch it off for departure.

The time difference between Australia and Avali meant he arrived as the sun was setting. As the plane descended through pink cotton-candy clouds, he caught sight of the island below, with its mountains and beaches painted gold by the rays of the setting sun. The breath he didn't realise he'd been holding released. For all the weight Avali put on his shoulders, it was his home. That sense of rightness settled in his gut as he stepped off the plane to be greeted by the island dancers, and the rhythm of the drums and the familiar movements called to him until he dropped his bag and joined them. His hips swayed as he tipped his head back to the fading light and let out a cry of joy. As the song drew to a close, the performers moved away towards the air-conditioned airport to reveal a tall man leaning against a luxury vehicle.

The other man caught Manu's eye over the rim of his high-end sunglasses.

"Bit stiff there." He spoke in Avalian, and the rounded vowels of his native tongue washed over Manu like waves welcoming him home.

Manu picked his bag up off the tarmac and threw it towards his brother. "I just played eighty minutes of footy," he replied in his first language. "Let's see you do better. Isn't twenty-eight when the arthritis starts to set in?"

Aleki snorted, slinging the sports bag into the back of his car. "I'm doing yoga twice a day to stay limber enough to meet my wife's second trimester needs. You wish you had this kind of hip flexibility. I could dance for dollars down at the night market if I wasn't busy running the country."

"Bit presumptuous to refer to Stella as your wife," Manu commented as he slid into the car behind Aleki. "There's still time for me to lure her away with my winning smile and natural charm."

"Well you'll have to be quick to make your play. We're getting married tomorrow."

Surprise danced through Manu's blood. With the exception of proposing to Stella within mere hours of learning he was going to become a father, Aleki did not make rash decisions. The responsibility of being an heir had influenced every choice he had ever made, and a quickie shotgun wedding was so far from the public's expectations of a royal marriage that Manu couldn't remember it ever having happened in Avalian history.

"What's the rush? Surely you can't have knocked her up twice."

His brother's mouth thinned in a firm line. "I'm tired of

waiting. There will always be a reason to delay the full three-day ceremony. Last week I came home from Parliament and she'd sent the staff home and had a traditional Avalian feast waiting for me, because it was Mother's birthday and she knew I would need some quiet time to recharge. And I just looked at her and knew I wasn't going to wait any longer to make her my wife."

Manu nodded slowly. He'd spent the night of their mother's birthday running laps on the Knights' track because Clare was working late and he hadn't had the nerve to ask her if she'd be willing to hang out with him on a non-Tuesday night.

"Still," he felt obligated to point out, "asking a five-month pregnant woman to pull together her own wedding in a week seems a bit cruel."

Aleki smiled, a quick tense curve of his lips that betrayed his nerves. "I didn't. I asked Jessie, her business partner, to do it. Stella doesn't know. I'm going to surprise her tomorrow."

Manu stared at his brother for a beat, then threw his head back in laughter.

"It's not funny," Aleki grumbled.

"You're planning the wedding of your wedding-planner fiancée in a week without telling her?" Manu chuckled. "I can't wait to see her face."

"I'm sure it will be awash with pleasure," Aleki replied loftily.

"You'd better bloody hope so."

"Moving on." His brother glared at him. "You're having a good season."

"You've been watching?" This time he didn't try to hide his surprise.

Aleki shrugged. "We stream your games. How's the knee?"

He hesitated. Aleki carried a lot of unnecessary guilt about his injury and Tua's death, given the fact the reporter who had caused the accident had been looking for information about Aleki at the time. "It's as good as can be expected," he finally said gently.

Aleki nodded once.

"And everything else? How are you finding Auckland?"

"I like it." Manu surprised himself by saying the words. Aleki spent a lot of his time in New Zealand working on his youth pathways programme, so Manu knew he was familiar with the different cities. "It's not as fast-paced as Melbourne was. I like the team, and despite their dire history, we seem to be doing pretty well. We're one game away from making the quarter-finals, which seemed unbelievable a few weeks ago."

Aleki snorted. "Yes. It did How is your living situation? Have you worn the angry scientist down with your tenacious positivity yet?"

Manu dropped his gaze, a smile spreading across his face. "She seems to have come around to my charms, yes."

"Oh gods." Aleki sounded horrified. "You're sleeping with her."

Heat flushed Manu's cheeks and he futilely wished his skin was dark enough to hide his blush.

"It's not serious," he blurted, and Aleki scoffed. "Sure it's not. You've broken your self-imposed vow of celibacy for a girl you've just met, is all."

"You're one to talk," Manu offered lamely in response. "You knocked Stella up during a one-night stand. At least I don't have to worry about that."

"How do you know?" Aleki countered as he turned into

the long driveway of Manu's Avali home. Manu's parcel of land - part of their mother's legacy - was on the northern part of the island, and the familiar craggy face of the volcanic black rock cliffs under which his house sat welcomed him home as surely as an embrace.

"We use condoms. My condoms," Manu snapped, his brother's hypocrisy grating on him as they approached his large island-style house, with its bamboo cladding and thatched roof balancing the modern whitewashed walls and flat stone steps that led up to the entrance. "And she has a contraceptive implant."

"So she says," Aleki grumbled, pulling to a stop on the gravel drive.

"It's in her arm, Aleki. I've felt it. Pregnancy is not a concern. She ... she doesn't want children." His last words came out quieter and he winced as he felt Aleki's gaze move over his face.

"Oh." His brother paused for a moment, before reaching out and clapping him gently on the shoulder. "Probably best it's not a long-term thing then." His voice was kind, and the words left unsaid cut through Manu. "Now," his brother continued with forced joviality, "let's check out your closet. Gotta look your best for my big day tomorrow."

Manu swallowed his discomfort as they got out of the car, Aleki claiming his sports bag from the boot and swinging it over one shoulder. "Calm down, brother. You don't want me looking too good, or Stella will see her mistake in choosing you."

Aleki grinned back at him easily, and Manu relaxed until his brother spoke. "She's not going anywhere. You're no competition to me, Manu."

Despite his brother's light-hearted delivery, the

comment stuck in his chest, the truth in the words a sliver of glass pinching at his heart. No matter what he did, he could never compare to Aleki, to his natural ease with politics, law and finance and with the day-to-day minutiae of running a country. The best he could hope for was to be remembered as a great player, a sportsman who brought pride to his country, whose efforts contributed to essential welfare services, and most importantly, allowed Kai to follow his dreams, the way his father Tua had been denied. Winning a rugby league championship would allow him to do both.

"I know," he murmured, following his brother up the steps. "Believe me, I know."

He moved past his brother to unlock the door and disable the alarm, serenity soaking through him at being home and back in his own house. He let Aleki veto several excellent outfit suggestions before they settled on a grey jacket with subtle traditional patterns on the lapels, a matching lavalava and a royal blue shirt for his wedding outfit.

Manu hung the outfit on a separate hook in his walk-in closet ready for steaming and returned to his bedroom, where Aleki was lounging on a low-slung rattan sofa and tapping out an erratic beat on the arm with his fingers.

"Nervous?" He took a seat next to his brother, the familiar piece of furniture enveloping him like a hug.

Aleki shot him a look from under his lashes. "Not about tomorrow." The other man hesitated. "I'm nervous about telling you something."

Manu straightened, apprehension sliding under his skin. "Are you okay? Is Stella?"

"We're fine," Aleki assured him. "But Dad had a health scare recently. Chest pains, loss of breath. He refused to let us tell you because it wasn't serious, and of course, we had to keep it hush-hush to avoid the people finding out."

Manu nodded slowly. His father had always been obstinate, and both he and his brother had their own issues with their father. Manu knew his father had certainly hoped for more from his second son than a high school dropout with a career running headlong into other men - his father's words. "He's okay now?"

"He's okay," Aleki replied slowly. "But he mentioned something when the pain kicked in. It's about Oliana."

That got Manu's attention. At twenty-three, their cousin Oliana was the baby of their family. Unusually for Pacific Island families of a certain generation, both sets of their parents had only had two children each. Aleki and Manu's mother, Tatyana, passed away when Manu was three, and King Tama's grief explained why they didn't have any younger siblings, but Manu had never considered why his maternal aunt and her husband hadn't given Sio and Oliana any more siblings.

"What about Oliana?"

All of them were a little protective of her - being the youngest and the only girl had set her up for some pretty heavy chaperoning when he was still living in Avali. Not that she needed it - Oliana Maiava was the perfect Pacific Island woman. She lived at home and cared for her parents, worked part time at one of the island's preschools and volunteered teaching reading to adults who had recently had their sight restored. Fear clutched in his chest. If anything were to happen to her ...

"She's fine." Aleki assured him, and the tightness eased a little. "It's just ... it seems she's not actually our cousin after all. She's our sister."

The words didn't register for a second. Then they

landed, one after another, with stunning precision. He couldn't breathe, couldn't think. The familiar setting of his living room faded away under the leaden weight of his limbs, the heavy beat of his pulse in his ears. When the blanket of shock thinned enough for him to fight his way out, he blinked rapidly to find Aleki still sitting there, his mouth in a grim line.

"Explain." Manu croaked, his brain clicking into gear and whirring as he processed the multitude of meanings that could be connected to Aleki's statement.

His brother let out a sigh "She's our sister. Our full sister, not that it matters."

Manu tilted his head in acknowledgement at that. Family was family in the Pacific. There were no differences between a first cousin and a sixth, between a sister with fifty percent share in their DNA or one hundred.

Aleki continued. "That's how Mama died - in childbirth with Oliana. According to our father, under the influence of near death, he asked Auntie and Uncle to raise her because he was too heartbroken to care for an infant. And then later," Aleki shrugged, "she just reminded him too much of Mama."

"You believe him?"

"I asked Auntie. She confirmed it."

"Fuck." Manu sat back in the cushions, his hands on his head. "Oliana. Of course. Oleander." The Avalian name was a translation of the name of the flower that could cause death. "Twenty-three years. And Sio doesn't know?" Their cousin adored his little sister. Family members adopting children when their parents were unable to care for them was common practice in Avali and other Pacific Island nations, but gods alive, everyone usually *knew* about it. Certainly he could never remember it happening in a royal family before. *King Tama and his infinite wisdom ...*

Aleki shook his head, distracting Manu from cursing out his father internally. "Just us, Auntie and Uncle. Sio would have been too young to remember. Just like you were too young to really remember Mama, and I was too young to remember the pregnancy."

"Fuck." Manu breathed again. It seemed appropriate. He closed his eyes, resting his head on one plush cushion. *Fuck, fuck, fuck.* Not only had the news left him feeling like he'd been sucker punched, but the devil of self-doubt that had plagued him since landing here now openly danced on his shoulder.

Oliana was *perfect.* She was the young woman the parents in the villages held up as an example to their daughters. *"Why can't you be more like Oliana? See, she helps her poor mother clear the leaves on the taro patch."* He'd heard it himself more times than he could count, snippets of praise for her as he, Tua and Sio ran through the village with their balls on the way to the park.

That praise rang in his head now, circling in a lazy tornado and mixing with the ever-present anxiety he felt about not living up to Aleki's reputation. *This* was why he didn't come home often. Bad enough to have one sibling that made him feel like a bridge troll intellectually. But to have two? And be sandwiched between them? He'd never escape comparison. Manu Esera, royal disappointment. He might as well print it on business cards.

"You okay?" Aleki's voice cut through the maelstrom of self-pity swirling in his brain.

He took a deep breath and opened his eyes. "Yeah. Just spiralling."

"Well, snap out of it. You're going to see her tomorrow

at the wedding and I don't need you hyperventilating at the sight of her."

"You're going to tell her?"

"Not tomorrow." Aleki looked aghast. "It's a *wedding*. Hardly the time. When do people normally drop massive life-changing bombshells that fuck up entire family dynamics?"

"Christmas?"

"Seems a bit far away. Waiting too long is just a dick move."

Manu exhaled through his nose. "You must have a plan." Aleki usually did.

His brother nodded firmly. "We'll tell her after your season finishes. Both of us. We can sit her down and tell her together."

"What then?"

Aleki sighed. "Then we announce it publicly. And we work on learning how to be a family again, in a different way."

Manu nodded, his mind already skipping forward to the field day the press would have. The heir, the spare and the perfect princess. If he didn't manage to get a championship medal soon, his name would barely warrant a mention on his siblings' Wikipedia pages.

More cardio, he reasoned, as Aleki nattered on about the strategic unveiling of their secret sister to the world's media. *More cardio and more game time. I just need to do more.*

FOURTEEN

"What the actual fuck just happened there? Why did they get a reset?" Clare squinted at her laptop screen and hoped for a replay so she didn't have to pause and go back. It was bad enough she was furtively watching sports at home alone on a Monday night. She had specifically finished work early so she could brush up before Manu returned home from his surprise visit back to Avali.

"Clare?" Manu's voice came from behind her. "Why are you watching the 2015 Grand Final?"

Shit. Not furtively enough, apparently.

"Because Jeremy from work said it's the best game he's ever seen."

She heard the air expel from his lungs in a sharp puff.

"No, lo'u alofa. *Why* are you watching it? Why are you watching any game?"

Heat rose up Clare's chest and flooded her face. She swallowed thickly. "Uh. Because it's your job."

"My job?"

She nodded, eyes still fixed straight ahead at the wall. "You, um, you like it. You're passionate about it. I thought it would be nice to learn the rules. And then, then I could ask you about it. We could talk about your day."

"You're watching league so you can ask me about my day?" The words were slow and drew across her heated skin like ropes of molasses, but without looking back at him as he approached, she couldn't determine whether he was pleased or thought she was nuttier than a barn bat.

"Yes."

A puff of warm air skimmed across the back of her neck, sending a shiver running down the length of her spine.

"You" - the brush of lips against her C_4 vertebrae punctuated the word - "are the sweetest thing I've ever seen."

A smile tugged at her lips. "Smooth talker."

"Mean every word." Manu's thickly muscled arms wrapped around her and she leaned back against him, tilting her head so he could nuzzle at the sensitive skin of her neck.

"How was Avali?"

Manu sighed, sending a gust skittering across her collarbone. "Complicated. But good. My brother got married."

Clare turned her head to capture his eyes. "I didn't know you were going home for a wedding."

"Neither did I. It was a surprise." He dropped a kiss on the top of her head and stood. "Do you want to go to the pub for dinner? I can't be bothered cooking anything."

"Mmm, please." She stood, stretching. "So, a new sister, huh?"

"What?" Manu ripped his gaze from her waist, where she could feel the cool winter air on the gap between her black top and jeans, to pin her with the intensity in his eyes.

Clare lowered her arms. "Your brother got married. You have a new sister. Well, in-law, I guess," she continued when he just stared at her. "What's she like?"

Manu blinked, shaking his head slightly. "Stella? She's great. Exactly what Aleki needs. And she's giving me a niece. What more could I ask for?" His face softened, excitement shining in his eyes. "I can't wait."

"She's pregnant?" Clare moved to walk past him, and he linked his fingers with hers as she passed, which allowed her to tug him towards the apartment entrance.

"Yeah." Manu's smile could have lit the dimly lit hall-way. "They announced the sex at the reception. Aleki said Stella had some nonsense in her head about all Avalian men wanting boys. But a baby girl? What a blessing. Well," he continued as she dropped his hand and shrugged into her green coat, "we've never had one before."

A shadow passed over his face, his dark eyebrows tugging together as he reached for his own coat. Clare waited while he zipped it, self-pity swirling in her stomach as she turned his words over in her head. How lucky to be that baby, to have people looking forward to her arrival, to all of the joy and love a little girl could bring. Not all daughters were considered blessings, and a sharp pang pierced her, a pricking behind her eyes at the sudden stab of jealousy she felt for an unborn infant, for the very idea that it was wanted in a way Clare had never been.

Stop it, she reminded herself firmly. *You're used to people being happy about pregnancies. That's why you do what you do, because you know those people want their babies*. Still, the thin edge of pain lanced her temples as her thoughts grew big and unwieldy, spreading out and multiplying - thoughts of little dresses and bows, of playhouses, and worst of all, of Manu smiling down at a little pink bundle in his arms, pride suffusing him.

He'd be such a good dad.

She swallowed thickly, pushing the vision away. "Is, uh,

is that something you're interested in? Having kids of your own?"

"Of course."

Of course. Like there was something wrong with anyone who felt differently.

"Family is everything in the Pacific," he continued, unaware that the small golden ball of hope she'd been carrying around in her chest was slowly shrivelling away. "Even if you don't know a person as well as you should, even if you didn't know they were family. Blood is blood." He nodded emphatically, punctuating his declaration with more passion than she'd ever seen in him outside of the bedroom or the field on game day.

"Oh. Right. Yeah." Clare nodded, an ache spreading out over her ribcage like a bottle of spilled wine staining everything it touched, the shiny delight of seeing him and holding him fading into shadows. She fiddled with the button at the hem of her coat. "Uh, should we go eat then?"

Manu shot her a concerned look, his recent intensity shrinking back until the air between them was almost normal again, not tight with words like 'babies' and 'family' and 'blessings' ballooning in the space and stretching at the edges of the delicate balance they'd found. He reached out and claimed her hand again, dropping a kiss on her palm. "Good idea. Let's eat."

Clare let him lead her out the door and down to the pub, where she ordered a steak meal and he ordered a lamb salad and looked at her raspberry lemonade as though it was the Beverage of Doom but didn't say a word about it.

After dinner they went back up to the apartment and snuggled on the couch under her favourite cream blanket while Manu explained some of the finer points of the 2015 Grand Final game. Then to bed, where they held each other tight, tighter than necessary, while they moved together, warm and slick, panting each other's names into the darkness as they rose and fell into the madness and passion and heady emotion of good sex.

And throughout it all the grey hole in Clare's chest - where once the golden light had lived - pulsed with the echo of Manu's words in each dull beat. *Family is everything. Family is everything. Family is everything.*

Family was the one thing she would never be able to give him.

The reminder was stark. He was only hers for a short time. She'd have to make the most of it.

———

THE SMELL of Italian food hit Manu as soon as he walked in the apartment door, but it was the sight of Clare in black lace underwear and a frilly pink apron that stopped him in his tracks.

"Honey, you're home!" Her smile was devastating.

Manu growled low in his throat and threw himself at her, tackling her gently around the waist and carrying her halfway across the open space to drop her on her back on the couch while she squealed with laughter. He couldn't help it. She'd been busy since he'd returned from Avali. Late nights at the office, rolling in just before midnight sometimes. She'd sent him a couple of pictures at his request – one in scrubs in a lab, one surrounded by empty coffee cups and a mountain of paperwork, but having her here in front of him, in all her soft, lemon-scented glory made his heart beat faster.

"I've never seen such enthusiasm for lasagne before,"

Clare gasped as he licked a hot stripe up the side of her neck.

"Fuck lasagne."

"Sacrilege," she cried.

Manu lifted his head and nipped at her bottom lip. "I'm not feeling very pious right now, lo'u alofa, and I don't think you are either. This outfit was not made with chastity in mind." He plucked at the lacy strap of her bra, soothing the snap with gentle lips.

Clare smiled up at him, the warmth in her grey eyes reaching into his chest and soothing all the rough edges that worried at him day and night. The stress of Oliana and what her true parentage meant, not only for the country but for him. It wasn't enough that he was already compared to Aleki and found wanting by most of the Avalian population, now he had a perfect younger sister closing out the ranks. He felt like the disappointing filling in the world's most perfect sandwich.

There was also the adrenaline from winning tonight's quarter-final and the stress of finals footy, which he'd never expected to see this year. He'd spoken to an old Giants teammate tonight after the game and finally admitted to himself that if he truly wanted a championship, he needed to give his all to the Knights. They were only one game away from the Grand Final now - he'd met his end of the deal with Harro and the Knights were having their best season in a decade. Any faltering, even subconsciously, could throw off his whole game. Even if the Giants came crawling back with a three-year contract tomorrow, he couldn't afford to think past this weekend, and hopefully the next. He was a Knight now, through and through. And he could be a champion in as little as two weeks if they kept up their solid performances. He could have it. Everything

Tua had dreamt of. Everything Tua had deserved. Manu could earn it in his place - for his family, for Kai.

The soft stroke of Clare's fingers down the front of his post-game shirt and tie pulled him back from the grimness of his thoughts.

"Well if it's sin my man wants, I'm sure I can provide," she breathed, and Manu almost embarrassed himself as her voice wrapped around him as snugly as her hand wrapped around his hard and aching cock.

Wriggling out from under him - no mean feat, but admittedly he was distracted by the shift and play of her breasts under the apron - she settled herself on his lap, soft thighs either side of his thick ones, draped her hands around his neck, and began playing with the short curls that had escaped the length of his braids.

"Hi," she exhaled, a sweet smile painting her face.

"Hi," he replied, low and soft. "I missed you."

She blushed, the action itself a startling revelation of how quickly they'd fallen into this new pattern, this alternative way of being. The Clare he first tried to pick up in the pub would have been more likely to roll her eyes at him than maintain eye contact. Certainly he could never have imagined the pretty pink painting her neck and cheeks when she'd shown him to Tex's room that first night.

"It's only been a few days," she protested.

"Too long." Manu snaked his hands around to the curve of her butt and squeezed gently. "And I was looking forward to a good luck kiss today. Maybe you should come next week."

"To the game?"

"Yeah." She was frowning slightly, so he leaned in and pressed a kiss against her furrowed brow. "You can go in the box with the WAGs. There's free food, free drinks. A free pass to ogle me as much as you want."

Clare tilted her head thoughtfully. "I do like free food."

He chuckled. "That's my girl."

"I'll think about it," she said, and his heart kicked up a notch at the idea of his two Auckland worlds coming together. The Special Olympics day had been one thing, but the team box was something different altogether. He'd never invited anyone outside of family before. It meant something, and as much as he could feel their time together ticking down, she was beginning to mean something to him too.

Then she slid to her knees on the floor and the meaning of that made his dick weep.

"Are you—"

"Shhh," she interrupted. "Just relax, okay?"

Easy for her to say. A thin blade of tension thrummed from the base of his spine to his balls. His cock was rock hard, heavy with anticipation and desire. Not a single part of him was relaxed - every muscle, every nerve stretched tight as she worked his pants and underwear down his hips and evidence of his desire sprang free.

Then she wrapped her lips around him and he forgot how to breathe.

There were no preliminaries, no gentle teasing. Clare gave head the same way she did everything else - like a true overachiever. Firm suction, energetic motion, one hand cupping his balls as her middle finger stroked the sensitive patch of skin behind them gently. He couldn't take his eyes off her, the way each bob of her head revealed his trimmed patch of hair and the glistening root of his cock before she slid back down, lips and tongue and throat working in glorious tandem designed to drive him out of his mind. In an embarrassingly short time, he wrapped his fingers in her hair and tilted her head so he could see into her eyes.

"Clare, baby. I'm close. If you don't want me to come in that sweet mouth of yours, you need to stop now."

She looked up at him, flushed and beautiful, her full lips still wrapped around the head of his cock, the prettiest fucking picture he'd ever seen in his life. And she rolled her eyes.

That was it. His balls tightened and fire spread through his abdomen as he cupped her face in his hands and let go, sensations flooding him as he exploded into her mouth, the haze of dizzying relief underscored with a sharp edge of excitement, like his first time all over again. He tumbled through time and space on a messy, exhilarating high, barely conscious of the fact that Clare kept sucking, drinking every drop of him down gently as he settled back down to earth. He watched in wonder as she lapped the final sticky bead from him and crawled up to sit in his lap. Instinct guided him to wrap his arms around her and bury his face in the warm curve of her neck.

"You'll come next week? To the game?" His breath ruffled her hair, rough exhales forced out from lungs that suddenly seemed two sizes too small.

"Yes," she said, wrapping her arms around his wide back and squeezing. "I'll come."

FIFTEEN

"Shit, shit, shit." She was late.

Clare rushed down the hallway, grabbing at her red coat as she passed the hooks. She'd felt a little silly earlier, painting her nails a red that matched the Knights' team colours, but Manu had been so excited about her coming to the game when he was writing down the instructions on how to get to the box and who would meet her where to ensure she didn't get lost. She'd been to Knight Park before, of course. The stadium hosted concerts and events in summer when the league finished, but she'd never been into the inner sanctum. Throwing open the door, she stopped in her tracks as she came face to face with a blonde woman holding a key as though poised to let herself in.

"Oh." Surprise flitted across the mystery woman's face. "I didn't think anyone would be home."

"Excuse me?" Clare could hear the hostility in her own voice. Anyone with a lick of sense would have quivered in fear, but the blonde pocketed the key and extended her hand to shake. "I'm Dalton Meyers. Theo Miller asked me to stop by and perform a valuation on this property."

Clare's eyebrows hit her hairline. "What for?"

The other woman shifted uncomfortably, withdrawing her hand. "I believe Mr Miller is interested in putting the apartment on the market."

Shock flooded Clare, dropping heavy and cold in her gut. Icy tendrils curled outwards, wrapping their unwelcome fingers around her limbs. She stepped back from the door and fumbled in her pocket with stiff fingers to extract her phone. Dalton Meyers stepped past her and made her way down the hall as though she sent people into cardiac failure every day of the week.

Tex answered on the first ring.

"Hello?"

"What the fuck, Tex?" Clare exploded.

She could practically hear him wince down the line. "I thought you were going out."

"Well, funnily enough, I don't share my schedule with you for the express purpose of allowing you to stab me in the back. Things changed."

"Things have changed here, too, Clare." His voice was gentle. "There's a really good opportunity for me to work privately in London. But I would need capital. Nothing's set in stone yet. I'm just exploring my options."

Hurt sliced through her. "You didn't even tell me."

"I didn't want to upset you for no reason. It might not even work out."

"What are the chances it will?"

His hesitation spoke louder than his answer. "High."

Right. So she was definitely looking at homelessness then. She lowered her voice, avoiding eye contact with the nosy estate agent who wasn't even trying to pretend she wasn't listening at this stage.

"Are you that tired of living with me?" She tried to

frame it as a joke, but the crack in her voice splayed her out open despite herself.

"No, Clare Bear. But maybe it's not a bad idea for you to learn to stand without me for a bit. If I move over here full time, we won't be able to lean on each other the same way anymore." Tex's voice was calm, patient.

Horrified, it dawned on her that this was the voice he'd always used when she was upset. Like she was a child, and he was her parent. Not the sibling relationship she'd always assumed, but one of responsibility, of helping her see sense.

Holy fucking shit.

She was a burden. She was a burden left over from their crappy teenage days, and he wanted to be rid of her. Not explicitly, he'd never cut her out, she was sure of that, but certainly he was done feeling like he was taking care of her. She hadn't even realised. Hadn't seen it coming. Just like the Pritchetts when she was thirteen - everything had been trucking along smoothly and then bam! Goodbye, Clare. It's been fun, but it's time to get on with our real lives now. Mortification spilled over her like lava, hot and thick, clogging her throat.

"Right," she choked out. "Okay. Well, thanks for the advice I guess. And for the room while I had it."

"Clare, don't be like that—"

"I have to go," she blurted over Tex's sensible tone. "Plans and all that. Talk later."

She thumbed the phone off and jammed it in the pocket of her jeans. Dalton's navy heels were click-clacking over to the balcony door.

"Can you lock up when you leave please?" Clare asked the shoes, and from somewhere above them a murmuring assent came, heavy on sympathy. Jesus, what a mess. Even the real estate agent could tell she was barely holding it together. But then it wasn't every day you realised your best friend had been letting you stay in his spare bedroom in a decade-long version of a platonic pity-fuck.

Hot tears pricked at the back of her eyes all the way to the stadium, and not for the first time, she cursed the fact she didn't have her own car. Crying on public transport was a step too far. As soon as she jumped down from the bus at the Knights Stadium stop, she took a deep breath through her nose. Then, once the acrid scent of bus exhaust had singed her sinuses and exorcised the worst of her demons, she headed towards the giant concrete ramp that lead to the stadium.

The air was clearer above the traffic, and she took advantage of it, gulping in a crisp wintery lungful as she made her way to the main entrance. A gangly teenager in a suit took her up through elevators and hallways until he deposited her in a room filled with plush furniture, an array of refreshments and a dozen shiny, polished women who immediately fell silent and stared at her.

Cool. Just like the first day at all those new schools again.

Gritting her teeth against the anxiety rising in her throat, Clare made her way to the food table. *When in doubt, carbs.* She quickly selected a range of canapes, focusing heavily on the dessert selection, and turned back to face the room, intent on finding a corner to squash herself into until the game was over.

She didn't have a snowball's chance in hell.

Cara, who had apparently been hiding behind the wall of flat-ironed hair and tight-fitting Knights jerseys, popped up. "Hi Clare!"

"Hi," Clare mumbled, staring down at the toes of her black boots.

"Everyone, this is Clare," Cara announced loudly. "She's Manu's new flatmate and this is her first ever game."

"Welcome, hon," one of the beautiful people said. "I'm Lauren Hollis, Matt's wife." She held out her hand and just about scorched Clare's retinas with the diamonds on display. She awkwardly juggled her loaded plate to her left hand and shook the other woman's. *Soft. Very soft.*

"Come sit," Lauren invited, far more pleasantly than Clare would have thought considering the rumours about her and Hollis in the news. "Scooch over, Ingrid. Grab another chair."

The women rearranged themselves quickly, making space for her. Despite the large televisions mounted around the space, they were all gathered around tables at the long window that looked down onto the field.

"There he is," Cara nudged Clare with her shoulder and pointed down to a black and red body on the field. Even without the assist, Clare would have spotted him in an instant. His hair hung down to his shoulder blades in his game day braids, bouncing as he moved swiftly forward and to the left, and his heavily muscled thighs bunched with exertion. No other set of legs on the field came close, and she had a brief, glorious flashback of resting her cheek on one solid limb as she drank him down while he looked at her with wonder in his eyes.

A shiver ran through her, and she dragged her eyes off Manu long enough to see the knowing smirk Cara was giving her. Clare quickly stuffed a mini lamington in her mouth.

"What do you do, Clare?" Lauren leaned forward, a smile in her eyes, and Clare felt a brief stab of pity for the woman who was clearly a zillion times too good for her slimy husband. Chewing frantically, she swallowed down the lamington and took a drink of water from the glass someone had kindly poured her when she arrived at the table.

"I work at North Hope Fertility," she answered.

"Really?" Lauren cocked her head, one perfectly shaped brow lifted. "I've been there before. Are you a doctor?"

"A team leader. I run a group of lab technicians, nurses and admin staff to care for patients, and I work on creating and transferring embryos."

"Fascinating," Lauren began, but was cut off by a high-pitched squeal.

"Look, look!" Cara was slapping Clare's arm as she rose to her feet, eyes fixed down on the field.

Clare followed suit, her eyes tracking Manu as he bobbed and weaved, ball in hand, ploughing through the opposition players mere metres from the try line. He launched himself through the air, his strong body poetry in motion, reaching forward with the ball, which skidded across the ground at the end of his fingers and then bounced off forgotten as Manu leapt to his feet with his arms raised to the cacophony of cheers that echoed through the stadium.

The box was no different, cheers and squeals piercing the air, as women clapped her on the shoulder and applauded, but Clare couldn't move. She could only stare down at the man on the field, the man whose gaze was fixed on the box she stood in, a wide grin splitting his face. He pointed one finger up towards the box and she leaned forward, hand on the glass, heart in her throat, breathless with anticipation.

What she didn't anticipate was him being slammed

hard into the ground by a rogue tackle and lying unmoving in a crumpled heap under the goalposts.

MANU CAME to in fits and starts, black blobs swaying in and out of his vision as the cold, hard earth and the gentle tickle of grass against the back of his neck gave him clues as to what had happened.

Fuck's sake.

He'd been on fire too. Strong runs, evasive footwork. That gorgeous try Chalmers had set up. It was a thing of beauty. A symphony of time and space and the rich bounce of the ball rising up from the earth and landing in his hands like it belonged there. Sonnets should be written, songs should be sung about the perfection of that play. Downward pressure on the ball, right there, just a press of his hands to leather and leather to grass. Exquisite. And then he'd been on his feet, arms up for the roaring crowd, but searching the box for her. He'd seen her too, a single flash of red before the world had gone black.

"Esera. You alright?" It was Marty, one of the medics.

Manu groaned in response.

"Alright everyone, back up and give him some space." Some of the blobs in his vision moved. Huh. Actual people, then. "Let's see if we can sit you up."

Arms wriggled their way under his back on either side and Manu struggled to bring his upper body to a sitting position. "I'm fine, I'm fine," he muttered. Gods knew, he didn't want any of the medics under him if he lost consciousness again. A hundred and fifteen kilos of pure Avalian male landing on anyone would be akin to being trapped under a rhino. He could break them in half.

Slowly, slowly, slowly he got to his feet, the medics on either side doing an impressive job of holding him between them. He wavered slightly, gritting his teeth against the internal sway as he tried vainly to lock it down. The walk to the sideline seemed to take forever, the distance only enhanced by the supportive applause from the watching crowd. The clack of his boots on the concrete floor of the tunnel was a welcome reprieve.

Injury was part and parcel of the game, but ever since the car accident at nineteen, he'd had struggled with enduring so much as a calf strain under the eyes of the public. The reminder of pulling himself out of the car with his arms, one leg dragging uselessly behind him, while the media's lenses were snapping away at his pain, at the potential end of his career, instead of helping him, cut deep. Almost as deep as when he'd looked back and seen Tua's lifeless body, eyes open and dull, and his hoarse sobs and pleas to the gods had risen to a crescendo, but the snapping never stopped.

The Avalian press never printed any pictures, of course. The disrespect to the royal family and to the dead would have been too much. But the international press had no such scruples. People who'd watched, rather than helped, had made themselves rich that day while Manu had lost almost everything.

He let himself be steered past the locker room and into the examination room several doors down. He tried to perch on the bed, but nausea flooded his throat so he gave up and lay down, closing his eyes tight against the harsh fluorescence of the lights.

"Wake up, pretty boy. You know the drill."

Manu groaned at the team doctor's directive. Head Injury Assessments were a staple of the game - every player who received a cranial hit went through the same set of motions to determine their ability to continue with the game. The good doc was right, he did know the drill. Sitting up, he had just started touching his nose when the door flew open, the handle bouncing it back off the wall.

"What the hell?" The doctor jumped back, turning towards the noise.

Clare stood in the doorway, eyes huge, the rich red of her coat doing nothing to camouflage the fact that her face was several shades paler than normal. Behind her, Cara stood several inches taller.

"Hey, Greg."

"Hey, Cara."

"Forgive the door. It's her first time." Cara nudged Clare into the examination room. She stumbled forward, her gaze locked on Manu, running over him as if cataloguing every detail.

"You're okay?" Her voice was barely a whisper.

Warmth swamped his chest. "I'm fine."

"Well, we haven't actually determined that—" Doctor Greg began, and Clare's eyes shot to him as though she'd only just noticed him standing there. She frowned, puzzlement marring her already taut features.

"I know you."

"Do you?" Greg looked down, fiddling with his stethoscope.

"Yeah." She stared at him for a beat, then clicked her fingers. "Doctor Barry. You came into my work a few times. How's Mrs Barry?"

Doctor Greg cleared his throat, his gaze fixed on his shoes. "She left me, actually. After, um, after you talked us through the results of our tests. Pretty directly afterwards. That afternoon."

"Oh." Clare's brow furrowed, but her tone remained the same. "That's a pity."

Even through the throb in his head, Manu caught the incredulous look Doctor Greg levelled at her. "Yes, it is. Please excuse me. I'll be back to check on you shortly, Manu." The doctor hurried out of the room, shying around Clare and Cara as though they had leprosy.

Manu chuckled, laying back on the bed and flinging an arm over his eyes. *Gods, she really is bad at making people feel comfortable.*

"What did I do?" Her voice was closer now. The soft touch of her fingers sent shivers through his body as she gently traced the bold lines of ink on the arm covering his face.

"Sweetheart, that was the perfect time to practice your bedside manner with an actual patient. And you scared him off."

Above him, Clare stilled. "Nuh uh. He's probably just upset about his wife leaving him." A current of uncertainty ran through her words, and he caught her hand, bringing it to his face and pressing his lips to her palm in a soft kiss.

To his left, Cara cleared her throat, and when he cracked one eye open he could see her smirking at him from near the door.

"All good, Manu?"

"All good," he replied, swinging his legs off the table and sitting up. "Can you find Harro and tell him I'm ready to go?"

Cara arched a brow. "Is that what Greg said?"

"Yes." The lie sat heavy and foreign in Manu's stomach, but this was the damn semis. His dream of a championship sat within reach and he was almost dizzy with it, his muscles drawn tight and ready, determination pushing him to his feet.

As soon as Cara had left the room, Clare hooked an arm around his back. "Are you sure you're okay? That looked like a painful tackle."

Manu smiled down at her open, naive face. "I'm sure, lo'u alofa. Come on, you can walk me out."

She held his hand all the way to the end of the tunnel where he kissed her temple and jogged back out onto the sidelines. Harro snorted when he declared himself ready to go back out and directed him to the bench, where he remained for the rest of the game, but the combination of the Knights' eventual win and having Clare waiting for him after the final whistle was enough to distract him from his lingering headache. He wrapped an arm around her waist and lifted his glass of orange juice as Chalmers made the toast in the team bar after the game.

"To the Grand Final!"

SIXTEEN

Clare was waiting for Trish when she arrived at work on Tuesday morning. Given that Trish arrived at precisely seven fifteen every morning, when Clare was usually gulping down black coffee in her pyjamas several suburbs away, this was no mean feat. Trish knew that too, if her raised eyebrow was any indication.

"Clare." She stopped in front of her office door and whipped out a set of keys attached to a small pair of brass knuckle dusters.

"Are those legal in New Zealand?" Clare's surprise at Trish's choice of key ring distracted her from her mission. Not that she of the stuffed sperm could talk.

Trish blinked at her. "Can I help you with something?"

"Oh, uh, sure. I'd like to talk to you if you have a second."

Trish unlocked her office door and entered, flooding the doorway with artificial light as she flipped on the halogens. Clare took that as assent and followed her in, shutting the door behind her.

When they were seated, with Clare in front of the desk

and Trish lounging behind it like a queen, backed by her scary art, Clare continued.

"It's about the lab manager position."

Trish sighed. "I'm sorry, Clare, I can't talk to you about that until the shortlist has been finalised. I can, however, assure you that all current North Hope staff members who apply will be given the courtesy of an interview."

"It's not that." Clare shook her head. "I, um, I ran into an old client this weekend. And it really highlighted the concerns you had about me working in a managerial position with the public." She took a deep breath. "I'm not ready. I don't think I'll ever be ready, because it's just not who I am. I'm not Susie Sunshine and you're right, people do need that kind of hand-holding when they come in to see us. I thought I could be, if I studied it, practiced a bit more, but," she shrugged, "it just doesn't work that way."

Trish eyed her carefully. "So what are you saying?"

"I'm saying I'd like to withdraw my application for the laboratory manager position. In fact, I'd like to throw my support behind Hilary for it. I've been reviewing the data and I think she would be excellent in the position." She reached into the pocket of her Very Serious Black Coat and pulled out an envelope. "I'd like this letter of recommendation to be added to her application, if it's not too late."

Trish took the envelope, tapping the corner of it slowly against her bottom lip. "And what about you?"

Clare steeled her spine, sitting up straighter in her chair. "I'd like to investigate the opportunity to move full time to the scientific division. I like my team, I do. I'm just more suited to the lab, and I want to be able to spend more time working there."

"You're giving up your team leader position as well?"

The arch of Trish's eyebrows was the only indicator of surprise. Damn, she was cool.

"Yes," Clare was firm. "I know I'll be taking a pay cut, but I think I'll be happier there."

"Huh." Trish stared at the Korean bujeok on the wall, but Clare had the distinct impression she wasn't really seeing it. "You know, Doctor Ernshaw is over sixty now."

"Yes." Clare hadn't attended the lunchtime celebration the North Hope staff had thrown for him in autumn, but she had snuck into the break room and eaten some of the cake once everyone had gone back to work.

"It's very likely he'll be retiring in the next few years. It might not be a bad idea to have someone with some leadership experience in the scientific division in a second-in-command position. Probably at about the same pay structure you're on now."

Relief flooded Clare and she sagged a little under the weight of it. "That would be great. I mean, if such a position were to be opened, I would love to be considered for it." She hadn't been looking forward to the pay cut, but having lived with Tex for so long, her savings account was pretty healthy. And truthfully, she'd already considered Doctor Ernshaw's advancing age in the pros-cons list she'd drawn up to put off packing up her bedroom.

Fuck. Her bedroom. Well, technically the bathroom too. And the kitchen. She wasn't leaving her excellent diffuser behind in the living room either. If Tex wanted the energising aroma of lemongrass and basil to invigorate him in the mornings, he could go out and buy his bloody own.

The wound was still raw, a ragged hole that sucked oxygen in through her chest but didn't let anything out, instead trapping all her doubts and hurt inside where they snaked through her like poison. She'd got through a good deal of Saturday night focusing on taking care of Manu. Between his tender ribs and the ghosts in his eyes, he'd been an excellent distraction from her own problems, but as he'd spent most of Sunday in his room, she'd had no choice but to replay her conversation with Tex in every aching detail. Nothing she'd found had convinced her that her initial reaction was wrong. He'd used kind words - of course he had, he was a kind person - but the sentiment remained the same. So she'd turned off her phone, because the texts asking her to pick up the calls she let slide to voicemail were getting close to begging, and it was bad enough that one of them had lost their dignity to such an embarrassing degree this weekend already.

At least then she'd been able to concentrate on her job situation. It was no use looking at flats online if she didn't have an idea of what her income was going to be. The suggestion that she might not lose a huge chunk of her pay check was a welcome one. Lord knew, she'd never be able to afford her own place in the city, but a small studio out in the western suburbs was still within reach. She'd be looking online at options. Exclusively one-person options. If anything, this weekend had reinforced her reverse-Little Mermaid sensibilities regarding housemates.

I want to be where the people aren't ...

Less people meant less opportunity to be hurt. She'd had enough of that for a lifetime.

SOFT SOUNDS FILTERED into Manu's consciousness bit by bit. The tinkle of ice in a glass, the gentle pop of the refrigerator seal.

"I know you're there, lo'u alofa."

"I was trying to be quiet."

Clare's voice sounded nearby, and he opened his eyes to see her rounding the end of the couch. Three days after the tackle that had knocked the stuffing from him and a dull headache still persisted. He'd thrown back a couple of paracetamol and a litre of water after training then collapsed on the couch in a weak shaft of winter sunlight. He must have drifted off. The curtains were drawn now, a sliver of dark sky appearing at the top where the two swathes of fabric didn't quite meet.

Clare settled down beside him, curling into him like a cat and he drifted his fingers up and down her back, contentment wrapping around him like a blanket.

"How was your day?" She asked, warm puffs of air skimming his throat as Clare nuzzled closer.

"It was good." Manu dropped a kiss on the dark sheet of her hair. "How was yours?"

"Scary."

"Yeah?"

"Yeah." She looked up. "I withdrew my application for the lab manager position. And I resigned from my team leader position."

"What?" His shock was edged with hope. *Did she do it so she could find work in another city? With me?*

"I'm being reassigned to the scientific division. All lab work, all the time. The good stuff. Chromosomal abnormalities and genetic predispositions. Plus, you know, still making the embryos and stuff."

The ball of light in his chest deflated. "So, you're staying at North Hope, then?"

"Of course." Clare gave him a puzzled look. "I can handle a pay cut, but not unemployment."

"That makes sense." He drew her head back down to

his chest. *Stupid, Manu. She's a genius. She's not going to throw away her career to be a WAG and follow you across the Pacific league scene.*

Clare drew one finger across the lines of his tattoo, tracing symbols that represented mountains, shark teeth and spear heads across his forearm.

"How come you were napping? Isn't your default mode athleticism?"

"I'll show you athleticism," he joked. "Come into the bedroom."

She huffed out a soft laugh. "No, thanks. I'm still worn out from last night."

"From our *Great British Bake Off* marathon? Understandable. I had a headache. Just trying to sleep it off. At this point in the season, rest is as much a part of training as cardio."

Clare sighed gently. "I would be a supreme athlete if it came down to my ability to rest."

"Yes, you would, lo'u alofa. Are we going to the pub tonight?"

"No. You looked so peaceful doing your Sleeping Beauty impression, I called Cole from my bedroom earlier and ordered our meals to take away. They'll be ready at seven."

Over her head, he checked his smartwatch. "Five minutes. You want me to go pick them up?"

"Yes, please." She didn't move though, fingers still running absentmindedly over the ink in his skin.

"I have to get up to do that."

"Ugh." She sat up, pouting, and he leaned forward, capturing her lower lip in a kiss, letting all his fondness, *hell, his love*, for her sink through his lips into hers.

She was smiling when he pulled back, her pretty face

open and soft, and conviction settled into his chest like it belonged there. Like it was a part of his identity. *Manu Esera. Prince of Avali. Player of rugby league. Lover of Clare Trescott.*

"I'll be back in a minute," he assured her, heading down the hall. He was bent over his shoes, tying the laces, when he heard her call from the couch. "Oh, Manu! Can you please grab me a raspberry lemonade and a chocolate mousse too?"

"No problem," he called back, shaking his head slightly. As soon as the season was over, he was going to join her in that combination, the sugar and fat content be damned.

He jogged down the five flights of stairs, so that he wouldn't feel guilty taking the elevator back up, and headed towards the pub on the corner. Cole was behind the bar polishing glasses. He looked up when Manu walked in and lifted a large bag filled with takeaway containers onto the shiny wood. Manu pulled out his wallet and a brief argument ensued when Cole claimed he'd been ordered to put it on Clare's tab.

"She'll kill me," the blond bartender said. "The only reason she didn't shank me with my own steak knife the night you met her was because you were a stranger, and she was disgusted at you for hitting on her."

"I've hit on her a lot more since that night," Manu countered reasonably. "I should pay for that."

"Sort it out with her yourself, mate." Cole shrugged. "I'm not messing with my favourite customer."

Frustration twisted in Manu all the way back up to the apartment. There had been girls in the past who always seemed to want something from him, and he'd been trained from a young age to avoid them like the giant centipedes that populated the islands in search of feet to bite. But Clare was different. He'd never been with a woman so clearly determined to want as little as possible from him. How on earth was he supposed to woo a woman who wanted for nothing? Even his one in, helping her with her application for the lab manager position, was now a moot point.

He found her in the kitchen assembling plates, cutlery and the tomato sauce she poured on every food she could. Her eyes lit up at the sight of the food in his hands. "Finally. I'm starving. I didn't eat lunch."

He sighed. "That's not good for you, lo'u alofa."

She rolled her eyes. "Jeremy keeps wanting to eat with me. And I didn't want to tell him about the job situation. Not before I told you."

His heart skipped a beat. "You wanted to tell me first?"

"Well, yeah." A pretty blush painted her cheeks. "You were helping me work on it. It seemed only right. And I really do appreciate everything," she added quickly, peering up at him, her grey eyes huge and earnest.

"I didn't do it for appreciation," he growled, tugging her closer by her belt loop. "I would have helped you no matter what."

Still blushing, she popped up on her toes and pressed a kiss against his cheek. A chaste kiss, by comparison to the things they'd done together, but Manu's heart beat wilder and faster at the unexpected show of tenderness.

"Come on," Clare said, shifting back. "Let's eat."

He hoisted the bags onto the bench and turned to rifle through the medicine box on top of the fridge as Clare started to unpack them. Swallowing two paracetamol dry, he turned back to see her watching him closely.

"Are you still not feeling well?" Clare asked. Something about her careful tone sounded alarm bells ringing through the fog in his head.

"Nothing major." Manu forced a smile and moved towards the bench.

"What's wrong?"

"Just a little headache, lo'u alofa. Nothing to worry about."

"Right." She didn't sound convinced. "But you were also sleeping in the middle of the day. That's not like you."

His smile tightened. "I'm fine, Clare."

Her eyes skipped over him, not lingering but assessing. Then she shifted to the left a little, exposing the meals on the bench behind her. "What's missing, Manu?"

"What do you mean?"

"I mean, what's missing from this order?"

He skimmed his eyes over the plates of food. Lamb salad, steak and chips, a side salad. The same meal they'd eaten together at the pub for the last five weeks.

"Nothing's missing." He folded his arms over his chest. "That's the same order we always make."

"Right. But today I asked you to order me two extra things. Can you tell me what they were?"

Manu swallowed against the sudden dryness in his throat. Fucking tests. He hated tests, he always had, and this one seemed like it was designed to fuck with him. He could see it in Clare's eyes, the same look that had haunted his teachers' eyes over the years. An aching pity that meant she knew he couldn't answer.

"Lemon meringue pie," he blurted. "You asked for lemon meringue pie. They didn't have any."

Clare shut her eyes and took a deep breath. When she

looked at him again, the hurt in them almost pushed him back a step.

"Manu," she spoke slowly, like he was a skittish horse. "When were you going to tell me you're concussed?"

SEVENTEEN

Manu's laugh echoed around the kitchen, hard edged and artificial.

"I'm not concussed." His declaration was firm, clear. And a total lie.

"You are."

"No, I'm not." His voice rose, but Clare was shaking her head before he'd finished the sentence.

"Don't do that, Manu. Don't disrespect me like that. I have a physiology degree, I spent an eight-week placement in the neurology department of Auckland General studying brain trauma. All of the symptoms add up."

She reached out to place a hand on his folded arms, but he turned away, leaving nothing for her fingers to find but air.

"It's okay," she assured him quietly. "You can bounce back easily. Three weeks to recover and you'll be as good as new."

"Three weeks, Clare?" His glare pinned her in place. "Are you crazy? I don't have three weeks. I have *this* week. This is it."

She gaped at him. "You can't seriously be thinking about playing this weekend?"

"It's the Grand Final, Clare. Of course I'm playing."

"But your brain ... the contact. Manu, you *can't*." Panic rose in her as he stared her down. "It's not safe."

He shrugged, his eyes shifting to the floor, his jaw set in a stubborn line. "Nothing's safe. You could go to the gym one day and end up dying in a car accident. At least this way I know the risks going in."

"And you'll risk everything for it?" She hesitated, the words lingering on the tip of her tongue. *Fuck it.* "You'd risk everything you have for a stupid game?"

His head snapped up, eyes flashing. "It's not stupid."

"It is if you think it's worth your life, Manu!"

His jaw worked. "And that's what you think of me? You think I'm stupid?"

"No—" she protested, but he was still going, his voice laced with hostility she'd never heard from him before.

"Poor, stupid, Manu. Didn't finish high school, didn't go to university, just a dumb jock. Can't compare with his perfect prince brother, not as good as his sweet little sister, just chases a ball around for fun, huh?"

"You're not listening." Clare broke in, anger peppering her speech. *Why won't he* listen? "That's your shit, Manu. I'm not pretending I understand what it's like to grow up the way you did, with your culture and the pressure on you. But I can absolutely tell you, *as a medical professional*, that playing with a concussion endangers your life. And no game on earth is worth that."

"Some people don't even get the chance, Clare. Did you think about that?"

She softened, some of the fight draining out of her at the misery in his eyes. "I know what it means to you to do this for Tua, Manu. But I can't believe he would want you to play either. He was forced to leave the people he loved behind. Nobody's forcing you, but if you play, you're choosing that option all the same."

"I'm not leaving you, Clare." Impatience snapped in his voice. "You don't understand. You're not part of a team. People are counting on me to play."

"And what about me? I'm—" She hesitated, before ploughing on. "I'm counting on you too, Manu. A single tackle could leave you brain damaged or dead. You can't promise me that won't happen because we both know it would be a lie."

His beautiful mouth pulled to the side, sullen. "I'm doing this, Clare. I'm doing it for me, I'm doing it for the team and I'm doing it for Tua and Kai."

Nausea rose in her and she lost her sight for a moment as his words registered. As he laid out the things, the people, who were important to him. *Of course* she wasn't on that list, *of course* not. How could she have let herself believe, even for a moment, that she might be? She wrapped her arms around her torso, as though that might hold together the pieces of herself that were shattering in the wake of his words.

"Such a fool. Such a fucking fool." The words slipped out past her lips, whisper soft and heavy with self-loathing.

"Clare. Come on." Manu made a move towards her. "It'll be okay. I love you."

The words fell like a hammer and she stepped back, away from the power of them, away from the false, senseless, pathetic hope that they represented. Pain rose in her throat, tightening her airway and blurring her vision.

"No, you don't."

Manu scowled, thick brows dropping low over those

beautiful eyes. Eyes she might never see again. The thought tore at her insides, scraping her voice raw.

"You don't." She choked the words out. "You can't, because you'll leave me. It was bad enough when I thought you'd just be going to another team, another city. But this? You're okay with taking the chance that you'd leave me forever." Her voice rose, her fears amplified. Now that she knew, now that she'd had this, how could he expect her to be okay with him risking his life for a stupid fucking game? "People don't leave the people they love."

But they always leave me.

The thought taunted her, filling her head in crimson swirls that pressed against the backs of her eyes and pushed the tears that had been threatening down her cheeks in unchecked rivulets. She turned towards the hallway.

"And just so you know, I Googled your brother. I know all about his sex scandal, the parties and the women. I'm not judging, but you're crazy if you think he's perfect. You're every bit the man he is. The only person who doesn't believe that is you."

The air changed behind her, the electric heat of their argument solidifying into an arctic wind. "How dare you?" Manu's voice was low, hard. "You have no idea who he is, how hard he works, the measure of him as a man. How dare you talk about my family that way? You've never even had a family."

There it was. The final snick of the knife through her heart.

"No," Clare replied softly as she moved down the hall to get to the safety of her room before the thriving mess of her emotions swallowed her whole. "No, I haven't. And I never will."

EIGHTEEN

Having never lived with a girlfriend before, Manu was at a loss as to how to apologise to one. So he bought everything. Flowers, chocolate, ice cream, a blindingly expensive face mask. Even jewellery. Trudging home after practice weighed down by his packages, he felt a little like Tui Fiti from the traditional legend, who presented himself as an eel to Sina and hoped she would love him despite feeling he did not deserve it. Certainly, decapitating him and burying his head in the ground, as Sina had done to Tui Fiti to create the first coconut tree, did not seem outside Clare's capabilities. Especially given the cruelty he had shown her last night.

However, when he shouldered open the apartment door, ready to light candles, strew rose petals and atone for his sins, he found the place still. Silent. More still and silent than it usually seemed when she was at work. It took him a couple of seconds, turning circles in the living room, to work out why.

The diffuser was gone from the console table. The chunky cream blanket wasn't slung across the couch like it had been since the day he moved in. He backtracked down the hallway, still clutching his bags, his eyes cataloguing the missing rainbow of coats on the hooks by the door that had escaped his notice when he first came in. His pulse increased as he pushed open Clare's door.

Nothing.

The room was devoid of colour - the red duvet gone, leaving a stark white mattress on the bed. All the art and knick-knacks that he'd admired were missing. Even her clothes. Not a scrap of her Angel of Death wardrobe remained.

Fuck. He'd done it. He'd pushed her away, out of her own home even. Guilt twisted inside him. And worry. Where on earth had she gone? He'd never so much as seen her with another person in the time he'd lived here, with the sole exception of the ginger behemoth who had dropped her off drunk.

As though Manu's thoughts had summoned him, the front door opened and the redheaded giant wandered through. He stopped short when he saw Manu.

"Ah. You're here."

"I am. Where's Clare?"

"Not here."

They glared at each other, strangers in the hallway of someone else's house.

After several silent seconds, Manu sighed. "Look, I just want to talk to her."

"She doesn't want to talk to you. She was pretty clear on that point." He nodded towards the bags Manu was holding. "What've you got there?"

Manu held them out for inspection and Jeremy poked through the bags. "These she might want. I'll take them to her for you." He turned to go.

"Wait," Manu blurted. "I, I just ... I need to know. How is she?"

Jeremy turned an incredulous glare on him. "Well, she's holed up in my spare room, despite the fact she only just started talking to me a few weeks ago. So I'm going to go out on a limb and say she's not great."

"Are you ... are you interested in her?" The words spilled out despite his best efforts to keep them inside, the poisonous green of jealousy tainting the light hallway.

Jeremy raised an eyebrow. "Not really any of your business anymore, is it?"

Manu gritted his teeth against the possessive rage that spiralled through him. *Stupid fucking question, he'd have to be an idiot not to be. He's probably already seducing her.* The reminder from his rational brain that he had no claim over Clare in any way did not help.

"She can come back," he ground out over the roaring in his ears. "She should come back here. It's her home. I can get a hotel room."

"No shit you can, rich boy. But I don't think you're her only problem with this place right now."

When Manu continued to glower at him, Jeremy lifted a shoulder. "Look, her landlord is selling the place out from under her, and you're apparently determined to fuck your life up, so you can see how she might be sick of all the shit that's going on here at the moment. She probably just needs a little break." He shrugged again. "Or she's busy plotting how to poison your protein powder. No skin off my nose either way."

"I'm not ruining my life."

Jeremy rolled his eyes. He was nowhere near as good at it as Clare. "You suffered a traumatic brain injury last week and you're planning to play contact sport seven days later.

That's fucking your life up, mate. Our whole office agrees and we've all got the qualifications to say so." Shock flowed through Manu, and it must have shown on his face because Jeremy smirked. "Turns out the key to making Clare chatty is just to have you piss her off."

Manu ignored that. "I could die any time."

"You could," Jeremy agreed mildly. "Especially if you keep taking that protein powder. But you're more likely to do so if you play this weekend. Don't get me wrong, I'd love to see the Knights win. Being a Knights' fan is a study in constant disappointment. But we're used to losing. Losing you, though? Not sure Clare'd bounce back from that."

"You don't think we should find happiness in the moment then?" Manu challenged. "If life's short, shouldn't we fill it with joy?"

"Guess that depends on what joy looks like to you," Jeremy replied evenly. "If it's eighty minutes of getting run over by giant sweaty men instead of fifty years cuddled on the couch with someone you love, then nothing I could say is going to change your mind." He reached into one of the bags and fished out a pint of ice cream. "This is melted now. Lucky for you, you can fix that." He tossed it at Manu, who caught it one-handed, the chill of the cardboard identical to the chill in his bones. With a nod, the other man left.

Manu walked slowly back to the kitchen and grabbed a spoon, then sat on the couch and spooned up mouthfuls of cookie dough flavoured dessert as he rolled Jeremy's words around in his mind. For so long, he'd considered joy as being an activity - something he did. Playing league, hiking, swimming at the sliding rocks in Avali. Living his life the way Tua couldn't; the way even Aleki couldn't, constrained as he was by politics and business. It was the way he felt connected – both to Avali and to the silent vow he'd made

Tua. But something had shifted in the last few weeks without him even realising it. He'd had more fun fake dating Clare than he'd had summiting mountains. For the first time ever, league felt like a job, rather than an escape, for him. A job he was content to finish up each day so he could come home and watch documentaries on the couch with her. Spending time with Clare had become his version of happiness.

The realisation rocked him. How could he not have seen it coming? And, more importantly, what was he going to do about it?

For a brief second, he considered calling Aleki for advice but quickly dismissed the idea. Aleki didn't know Clare. And despite his brother's new-found enthusiasm for chatting about his feelings, he was bloody lucky he'd managed to snag Stella. Good personal relationships were not an Esera family trait. Gods willing, he hoped Oliana had more luck in that department. What's more, he'd made this mess himself. It was on him to fix it.

Determination blazed in his veins. He *would* fix it. True happiness was finally within his grasp and no way was he letting it slip through his fingers. That was the greatest honour he could bestow. On his country and his friend, yes. But also on himself. He deserved happiness. And after years of feeling like he wasn't good enough, suddenly, desperately, all he wanted to do was prove that he was.

THE DOOR to Jeremy's spare bedroom swung open and the man himself appeared.

"I come bearing gifts."

Clare rolled over in the small double bed and pushed a swath of tangled hair out of her eyes.

"What?" *Elegant, as always.*

"I saw Manu at your apartment. Distraught, of course, and rightly so. He bought you presents. I confiscated them, but if you don't want them I'm happy to take them off your hands."

"Don't be ridiculous." Clare sat up and reached out towards the bags. "Gimme."

Some girls shunned material attempts to win back their favour. Clare was not one of them. If anything, Manu should buy her more gifts to make up for breaking her heart. Maybe a pony, or a superyacht.

Jeremy flopped on the bed, narrowly missing crushing her tibia, and spilled the contents onto the comforter. They picked through the items together.

"Ooh, good taste." Jeremy held up a face mask. "You mind if I claim this one?"

"Go for it," Clare responded, opening a box of chocolates and immediately stuffing three in her mouth without even pausing to check the flavours.

The doorbell echoed through the small house and Jeremy groaned, rolling off the bed. "Must be the Thai."

He wandered out of the bedroom, and Clare rolled onto her back and stared up at the crown moulding as she chewed on a mouthful of chocolate-covered nougat. Jeremy had told her he'd inherited the house from his grandmother - apparently the only way he could get into the Auckland property market without selling a kidney on the black market. She wasn't looking forward to taking that step herself - it was nearly impossible to buy a place on a single income nowadays. Tex had been a genius to buy as young as he did. Mind you, fertility science was a growing field. As committed as she was to North Hope, it wouldn't be a silly idea to look at other regions with a lower cost of living in the long term. Maybe even the South Island.

"What the fuck are you up to, Clarity Sage?"

She jack-knifed up in bed. Tex stood in the doorway of the small bedroom scowling at her, his hands on his hips.

"What are you doing here?"

"You've been avoiding me. I came to talk to you."

"From *London?*" A thought struck her. "Hang on, how did you even know where to find me?" Nobody except Jeremy and his boyfriend, who had both taken time off work to help her move that morning, even knew she was leaving Tex's flat.

Tex snorted derisively. "You know what I do for a job, right?"

"Stalk me, apparently," she muttered. She was not appeased when he just shrugged.

"I want to talk to you. So I came to see you. Come on, Clare Bear. This isn't us. We don't break down like this." He crossed the room in a few short steps and sank down onto the mattress.

"I don't break down at all."

"Maybe it's time you did." He reached over and pushed her hair back in a brotherly gesture. "You've been holding your shit down for a long time, but you can't control everything."

"Like where I live?" She arched a brow at him.

Tex sighed. "I'm done with the army, Clare. It gave me what I needed when I joined, but I can't do it anymore. The things I've seen, the things I've been a part of." He met her gaze. "It's not good for me. I applied for my release last week."

"You used to talk to me about those things," she reminded him gently.

A half-smile tugged at his lips. "I used to be better at handling them."

"I understand. But I didn't like hearing about it from someone else."

"I know. I'm sorry I didn't tell you."

"It's okay." She paused. "I think I needed a push. You were right that it's time to stand on my own. In a way, you've been my safety net since we were kids. It would be nice to be friends without that there."

"Not just friends," Tex reminded her. "We're family."

"I've never been great with families."

Tex scoffed. "What are you talking about? I've been gone three months and you went out and got a whole new one. You're living in the house of some guy I've never seen before in my life. I practically had to promise him my first-born to get him to let me in, he was so protective of you. You're more loveable than you think, Clare Bear. As soon as you stop pushing people away, they come swarming in."

"That's not a family."

He shot her a scornful look. "That's exactly what a family is, Clare. You and I, we've been knocked around a bit and it fucked up how we see things. But there's no such thing as a perfect family. There's people who love you and take care of you, and those that don't. This might be hard for you to hear given what you do, but biology doesn't have anything to do with it."

As Clare tried to wrap her head around Tex's words, there was a knock at the door.

"Can I come in?" Jeremy's plaintive voice called from the hallway.

"Yeah," Tex responded, and the door edged open to

reveal Jeremy with a carafe of coffee, a bottle of Baileys and a selection of mugs balanced on a tray.

"I thought maybe you'd like something to drink. And then we can eat the rest of Clare's chocolates and talk shit about a certain royal rugby league star."

"Sounds good," Tex drawled, running his gaze over Jeremy. Clare poked him sharply in the ribs. "He has a boyfriend," she hissed under her breath. Tex made a face but stopped eye-fucking the big ginger lumbersexual.

She tried to concentrate as Jeremy poured spiked coffee and suggested a toast - "May he rupture something crucial in one of those magnificent thighs!" - but she couldn't help mulling over Tex's words as she drank the concoction down. All the work Manu had done to help her connect more with people had led her right here. To a pair of pseudo-brothers who had both proven within the last twelve hours that making room for her in their lives was a priority. If only there was a way she could do the same for Manu - give him the same sense of security she was feeling now.

"Hey, Tex?" she asked slowly, the idea forming in patches. Her best friend looked up from pouring more Baileys into his coffee. "Could you track down a prince's private cell phone number for me?"

NINETEEN

Manu was shitting himself. Pacing the corridor outside Harro's office, he ran his hands through his new, short haircut. It had been a spur of the moment decision to get rid of the long hair he'd had since his teens, the hairstyle he'd shared with Tua. He'd been feeling good about it until Chalmers had clapped him on the back with a sympathetic, "Break up haircut, huh?"

The sudden ding of a text message pierced the air and he slowed his pacing enough to pull his phone from his pocket and check it.

New message from Clare.

His heart leapt to his throat. Was she messaging to tell him she loved him back? To tell him she hoped he lost? To say she'd shoot him down with a horse tranquilliser if he so much as looked at his uniform?

None of the above.

Good luck tonight, Scarecrow.

He couldn't even imagine how much it had taken her to type that out, given her feelings on him playing. He messaged back warily.

Scarecrow?

You're outstanding on the field.

Manu groaned, even as lightness lifted his spirits. His girl had terrible taste in jokes, but damn she was cute. Resolve steeling his spine, he knocked briskly and pushed the door open before he could talk himself out of it.

Harro glanced up from his desk. Papers were strewn everywhere. Three monitors protruded out from the administration carnage, but Harro was hunched over his tablet, scrawling on it with a stylus. He ran his gaze over Manu.

"Nice suit. Why the fuck are you wearing it?"

Manu took a deep breath and steadied himself before he said the words that would change everything.

"I'm not playing."

Harro sat back in his chair and slowly folded his arms across his chest. Outside the office, the hum of the stadium waking up for tonight's Grand Final was swelling, an electric atmosphere. Inside the office, there might as well have been a hoar-frost on the carpet.

"Why do you say that?"

"I suffered a concussion in last week's game."

"You said you were fine."

"I lied."

Without taking his eyes off Manu, Harro reached over and pulled a phone handset out of a mountain of spreadsheets and training bands. Stabbing a few times at the pile where the rest of the phone must have been sitting, he held the handset to his ear.

"Send Barry down here."

He hung up, and they eyed each other for the eternity it took for Doctor Glen to arrive.

The doctor opened the door cautiously, took one look at Manu and swallowed hard.

"Barry," Harro barked. "Esera here reckons he's concussed."

Doctor Glen's eyes darted back and forth between them. "There was no evidence of that when I examined him last Saturday."

"You didn't examine me," Manu pointed out. "You got me to touch my nose, then my girlfriend came in and made you uncomfortable, so you left.' Saying the word girlfriend in relation to Clare felt like a risk, like there was every chance she'd jump out of a cupboard somewhere and yell, "I'm not your girlfriend, you dickhead," before kicking him in the shins and running away. Still, confidence was key here. If he believed hard enough that she'd come back to him, maybe she would.

Doctor Glen forced a laugh. "That's ridiculous. Of course I performed the full Head Injury Assessment."

"No, you didn't," Manu snapped, irritation pulling at his temples. "Stop trying to cover your own arse here and tell the truth. I'm not fit to play and if you'd bothered to examine me properly on Saturday you'd know that." He turned to the coach. "Have him check me now. I've got headaches, I'm fatigued but not sleeping well, I'm sensitive to light and I'm forgetting shit."

"Sounds like Grand Final nerves to me," Doctor Glen responded with a laugh, full of we're-all-mates-here bluster, and Manu was struck by the sudden urge to punch him.

Harro steepled his fingers in front of his face. "Wait outside, Barry."

Doctor Glen backed out of the room and the coach continued to stare at Manu.

"That all true?"

"Yes."

"I need you on that field."

"I know." Manu nodded. "I want to be on that field, believe me. It's the only thing I've thought about for years. But I won't put my life on the line for a trophy. I'm not asking you to let me sit it out, Coach. I'm telling you I'm not playing. And if they can't win it without me, then what kind of team are we really?"

"A different one than we were a couple of months ago." Harro nodded firmly, as if deciding something. "Okay. You've made your choice. And we're in the Grand Final, so I can't say you haven't held up your end of our agreement. I'll talk to the Board about getting you traded for next season."

"Don't." The word was out before Manu could stop it, before he even knew it was coming. But once it was out there, something clicked into place. "Don't," he repeated. "Maybe the boys will win tonight, maybe they won't. But I want to be with them when they win it next year."

The shadow of a smile pulled at the corner of Harro's mouth.

"You want to be a Knight now?" The question was silky, and Manu shook his head quickly.

"No, Coach. I *am* a Knight now."

Harro's smile spread into a satisfied smirk. "Well, okay then. Tell Barry to come in on your way out."

Manu left the office feeling thirty kilos lighter.

CLARE HAD NEVER KNOWINGLY MET royalty before. She wasn't a fan. Oh, Prince Aleki of Avali and his wife, Stella, were lovely, both greeting her warmly but refraining from hugging her. *Thank God.* Stella, who was in her second trimester, asked her and Hilary insightful questions about their job, and Aleki toasted the Knights' chances for a win with Tex and Jeremy over domestic beers. But it felt strange, the fact that actual royalty had jumped on a plane and flown halfway across the Pacific mere hours after her mildly bitchy voicemail suggesting it would mean a lot to Manu for his brother to support him in person.

Mildly bitchy correspondence was Clare's speciality. She'd perfected it working as a receptionist for a law firm while she'd studied. She didn't get to use it much for work, given the delicate state of mind of many of North Hope's patients, but she relished the opportunity whenever one of her team faced passive aggressiveness or outright rudeness from outside their tight unit. And despite the feeling of freedom that had been growing in her chest since she'd told Trish she no longer wanted to be a team leader, her team was tight. She'd had a hand in hiring and training most of them, and she was looking forward to going over the applications that had already started rolling in since Trish had advertised her position earlier this week to find the right replacement.

Aleki and Stella's invitation for her and her friends to join them in their box for the game had therefore been unexpected, but despite her immediate instinct to decline, she'd thought about it and decided that it presented a logical opportunity to move outside of her comfort zone, within clearly delineated parameters and therefore it would be foolish not to accept. Tex and Jeremy had jumped at the opportunity, although Jeremy's boyfriend had declined, apparently due to work commitments. She hadn't actually seen him since she'd moved into Jeremy's place earlier in the week. As a result, Clare had approached Hilary at work yesterday, heart hammering unreasonably loudly, and asked if she would perhaps like to join them as well. Four, she reasoned, was an excellent number for a friend group, and given the fact the Avalian royals were travelling as a couple, it would also make things easier for the catering team. Hilary had immediately and enthusiastically accepted her invitation and set about securing a babysitter for Grace.

But what was keeping Clare on edge - shifting uncomfortably in the plush seating and tugging at the sleeves of her new red sweater, bought especially for the occasion - was the way in which Prince-just-call-me-Aleki's sharp gaze kept finding and studying her. There was nothing sexual in his look, no heat or softening of his face, which was reserved for when he looked at his wife perched next to Clare on the arm of her chair in a black wool dress, tights and boots. Still, it was unsettling all the same to be the focus of such scrutiny. So no, Clare was not a fan of meeting royalty.

Nevertheless, she did her best to ignore him and was succeeding pleasingly well until the women's conversation about the medical uses for blood cells found in umbilical cords caused Stella to lift her head and call across the room. "Hey! Aleki!"

No waiting for him to finish his conversation, no meek dancing around for his attention. She asked for what she wanted and received it. Clare fell a little bit in love with her.

Aleki arched an eyebrow. "Yes?"

"We're storing our baby's cord blood. Did you know it can be used to help treat cerebral palsy? We need to investigate opportunities to offer this service on the island at a reduced cost."

"Whatever you like, fafine aulelei."

Stella smiled wide with obvious satisfaction. "Excellent." She returned her attention to Hilary and Clare. Hilary was looking at her like she'd just invented cheese. Clare suspected her own expression was similar.

"That's all it takes?" Hilary breathed. "My God, the efficiency."

Stella laughed. "Well, Aleki has been particularly interested in developments in the healthcare sector since we found out we're expecting. And being married to him does give me an in."

"That deserves another drink," Clare said, standing. "You want anything, Hilary?"

"A husband with the ability to implement medical policy?"

"Who doesn't?" Clare sighed dreamily.

The other women laughed, but Clare felt Stella's gaze on her, assessing. Not unlike her husband.

Her husband, who cornered Clare as she reached for another trio of ginger beers.

"Hello." His voice was as melodic as Manu's, the lilt of the Pacific Islands peppering his English, but lighter. It didn't hit her in her gut and stroke outwards until she was all but shivering from the warm gravel of his tone.

"Your Highness."

Aleki laughed. "I think we're a bit past that now, aren't we, Clare? Your voicemail put paid to that level of formality."

He grinned suddenly, and she saw it then, a glimpse of what he would have looked like without the years of responsibility carving themselves into the grooves of his face. He reminded her so much of Manu with that flash of teeth that the air caught in her throat and she choked, barely managing to avoid showering the heir to an entire country in spittle. She hadn't seen or heard from Manu since she'd left the apartment, the bags of treats notwithstanding, and the sharp ache of missing him had yet to dull. Even being here cut through her, knowing he was buried in the bowels of the stadium at this moment, strapping himself into his armour of lycra and hope for the coming game, and a continuing loop of what-ifs played in a reel in her head.

Aleki patted her back absent-mindedly and handed her a glass of water, politely ignoring her attempt to drown him in her DNA.

"How has Manu been?" His words were cursory, taking advantage of their shared link, but she heard the uncertainty underneath them. Pity shot through her, followed by a trail of anger. The perfect family and they still couldn't get their shit together enough to function.

There's no such thing as a perfect family.

Tex's words echoed in her head, and they made sense now. Here was one of the most powerful men in the southern hemisphere, asking her for information about his brother, information he should already know. Frustration licked at Clare because it was obvious, even to her, that these two men loved each other and were dancing around it. Love was too rare to be toyed with.

Manu said he loves you a little voice in her head whispered, and she pushed it away because that was different, that was sex and comfort and confusion, not the deep love of family.

"He's not good," she responded. "He's injured and he's playing anyway because he thinks he needs to prove something."

Aleki's eyes widened. "To who?"

"To you," she replied, giving in to an eye roll because,

really, class was a social construct and this man must have been dense as osmium not to know.

"Me?" The look on his face was almost comical. It might have been if his ignorance of the situation hadn't made the man she loved feel unworthy.

"Yes, you. He thinks you look down on him because of how he makes his money. He thinks your people don't take him seriously because his contributions come from balls and his body instead of boardrooms and backstabbing." She glared at Aleki - Death Glare Number Three. "He thinks he isn't cut out for anything more than this sport because he's never been given a chance to try. But he can do anything he wants. He's just too afraid to try in case he lets you down. So he sends money instead, and you appreciate the funding but not the way he gets it." Her breath punctured the air between them, hard and hot. "He thinks he has to prove something to you. And to Tua and Kai. So he's going out there tonight to do it. Even though it could break him forever." She picked up the ginger beers. "So yeah, to answer your question, he's been shit."

She turned, but a gentle hand on her arm gave her pause. She looked back to the prince, whose brow was furrowed but whose dark eyes were clear.

"I appreciate you telling me that. I needed to hear it. Men like us, families like ours ...' He shrugged. "Sometimes we forget why we do what we do. All of us. We get wrapped up in habits that are easy, but maybe not so healthy." His voice sobered. "I will make sure he knows how much we appreciate him and what he does for us. All of us. Fa'afetai, Clare. Thank you."

She nodded, then paused. "Fa'afetai means thank you?"
"Yes."

She hesitated again, the words tingling on the tip of her

tongue, a manic pixie voice in her ear, urging her on. *Ask, ask, ask.*

She cleared her throat, ignoring the heat climbing her cheeks. "What does lo'u alofa mean?"

Aleki smiled then, big and bright and a touch too smugly for her liking. "It means *my love.*"

Oh. Okay then. Right.

"They're running out!" Jeremy had to shout over the sudden swell of noise outside the box. Ignoring Aleki's smirk, she headed back to the group of chairs where the others sat. Scanning the tiny red figures down on the field, her heart in her throat from Aleki's revelation and her own nerves, she had to look several times before she realised what she was seeing. *Or not seeing.*

Turning towards the large screen mounted on the box wall, she watched as the commentators ran through the list of players for each team. And then Manu showed up on screen, his hair short and spiked, his cheekbones high and wide, laughing in a grey wool coat while talking to someone on the Knights' sideline. Even as her brain struggled to put the pieces together, and her vagina screamed at her to go to him, a banner appeared at the bottom of the screen. *Manu Esera Suffers Injury Before Grand Final, Replaced by Ivan Phillips.*

Her breath caught in her throat. Had there been another injury - a head knock during practice or Jeremy's curse of a strained hamstring come true? But the more she watched the screen, the more she noticed his demeanour - relaxed but focused, his eyes trained on the field even as he exchanged words with his companion. He didn't look like he was in distress. He just … wasn't playing.

Relief exploded out of her in a rough exhale. It didn't matter. It didn't matter why he wasn't playing, just that he wasn't. The weight that had been pressing against her chest all week loosened its hold. Only to slot back into place when she turned from the screen and found five pairs of eyes staring directly at her, all five heavy with speculation.

"Well," Tex said, a tiny grin tugging at the side of his mouth. "That might change the outcome."

TWENTY

Five minutes to go.

Manu breathed out, elbows resting on his jiggling knees, hands clasped tightly between his spread thighs. The game had been a nail-biter. Messy play dominated the Knights' first half offence, and coupled with their opposition's search for back-to-back championship titles, they'd been down twelve points at halftime. Through hard slog, guts and a couple of brilliant plays from Chalmers, they'd pulled their way back to a four point deficit. A converted try would do it, but right now they were down in the opposition end facing a wall of muscle.

The clock ticked down. Each second shaved off the digital scoreboard clock ratcheting tension higher in Manu's body until his muscles screamed. The crowd roared, on their feet - Victor Hewitt with the intercept, the big veteran battling down the field, crushing defender after defender under his boots and bulk and leaving opposition players scattered in his wake. It took three of them to take him down in a messy, brutal battle. The whistle rang, loud and clear, a penalty to the Knights.

Rangi Katu took the kick, sending it out downfield for the restart.

And that's when he saw it - the play appeared in his mind's eye, bright and clear as a summer's day. It was too late for earpieces - Harro would be on his way down from the coaches box already, full of gracious defeat or humble pride, whatever the next ninety seconds of play dictated. Grabbing a basket of water bottles, Manu ran out onto the field himself. The team were working themselves into position for the reset, Chalmers at the back. Manu tossed him a bottle of water from ten feet away. "I've got it."

"What?" Chalmers squirted the water directly into his mouth.

"The play. Give it to Hollis and have him double back and hand off to Zac." Zac Fearon was an outstanding player, but he'd been quiet all season. Nobody would be expecting it. Chalmers observed Manu silently over his upturned bottle, then nodded once.

Manu jogged back to the sidelines, water bottles bouncing in their basket, and faced the field. *Ninety seconds. That's all we need.*

In the end, it was perfect. The ball came up from the scrum, was passed out the line, a twist, a spin and a dodge later it was in the big centre's hands, five metres out from the line, not a defender in sight. The opposition were still focused on Hollis drifting to the left as Zac angled right, his legs driving into the grass as he threw himself towards the line and slid, the ball skidding across the white paint.

Rangi had the conversion set up in seconds, the air in the stadium silent and still as Knights fans held their collective breath. And then it was sailing, sailing, sailing between the goalposts and the cheers were deafening.

Manu rushed onto the field, elation giving him wings on

his feet. He threw himself into the crush of bodies, revelling in the contact, the press of sweaty shirts and sticky champagne rain as cheers echoed in stereo between the crowd and the team. He found Chalmers in the mess and they came together like a clash of titans, arms holding each other close as laughter bubbled over.

"You bloody legend," Manu hollered in his ear. "I fucking knew you could do it."

Chalmers pulled back enough to clasp their hands together tightly. "Not without you, brother. Not without you."

He was pulled away by the crowd in a wave of backslapping and congratulations. Manu dished out a few of his own, riding the high of being part of a Grand Final championship team for the first time. He and Hollis even ended up with their arms around each other when the team gathered in a circle as Rangi performed an impromptu celebratory breakdance.

Eventually the organisers had everything set up for the presentation and the antics settled down as speeches were given and the medals presented. Manu walked on air across the makeshift stage as his name was called, shaking hands in a haze that only dissipated as the weight of the championship medal settled around his neck. He closed his eyes and sent a quick prayer heavenward to Tua.

Mo oe, lo'u uso. *For you, my brother.*

The serenity of finally having achieved the goal he'd worked towards for so long held through the team photo and the requisite media interviews, where he accepted kind praise on his impact on the team's trajectory since he'd arrived and assured reporters he'd be fit and healthy for preseason training in three months.

The team eventually made it back to the changing

room in various states of undress, some team members holding bottles of champagne loosely in their fists while belting out 'We Are The Champions' with the hard percussive beat of cleats on concrete and palms on steel keeping time.

Through the crowd he spied a flash of grey wool and red jersey and then Aleki was there, sweeping him up in a tight embrace and lifting him off the ground. Aleki shouted praise in his ear, barely discernible over the volume of off-key Queen lyrics, but Manu was giddy with his brother's presence and pride.

"You came," he shouted, after Aleki had plopped him back down to earth with a lot less dignity than he'd lifted him, and his brother's eyes twinkled.

"Clare told me I had to," he yelled, and Manu's heart skipped a beat. "Stella's outside," his brother continued as the music around them morphed into twenty grown men scream-singing Katy Perry's 'Roar' with fervour.

Manu allowed his brother to tug him out of the changing shed, and he embraced his sister-in-law, patted the bump where his niece grew and listened to Aleki and Stella dissect the game until his patience gave out.

"You talked to Clare?" He interrupted Aleki's description of the final play unapologetically.

Stella snorted and her husband shot her a quelling look.

"Yes," Aleki replied. "She called me - on my *personal cell phone*, I might add - and told me I needed to get my arse on a plane and come watch my brother achieve his lifelong dream."

Manu worked to untangle the knot of emotions in his chest - love, embarrassment, a healthy dose of gratitude. "But I didn't play."

Aleki shrugged. "She seemed as surprised by that as the

rest of us. As far as we all knew, you were supposed to be on that field."

"I didn't play for her." The words were out before he could stop them. "She didn't want me to. She said it wouldn't be safe."

Aleki clapped a hand on his shoulder. "She was right. I'm glad you listened to her." He hesitated. "I'm glad you have someone here who cares about you."

"I don't think she does." He kicked the tunnel floor morosely.

"She does." Aleki's voice was firm, unwavering. The kind of voice he used in Parliament. "And if you care about her, you probably need to let her know."

"I have." Manu gritted his teeth, the swell of celebration fading in the shadow of his brother's censure.

"Try again. You're not the kind of man to give up when you want something, Manu. Neither of us are. Go get your woman."

Manu nodded slowly as Stella wrapped her arm through Aleki's and whispered in his ear.

"We've got to head back to the airport. I'll call you tomorrow," Aleki promised. "I want your opinion on this new climate change initiative we're drafting."

Unease knifed through Manu sharply. "I don't really know anything about that."

"Doesn't matter," Aleki shot him a grin over his shoulder as he and his wife departed. "I want to know what you think. You're my brother. I trust your judgement."

Manu stood in the tunnel for a long time after Aleki and Stella left, mulling over his brother's words. He was finally part of a winning team. He'd fulfilled his unspoken promise to Tua. He had his medal. But he was missing his prize.

Time to go get my woman.

CLARE POKED at her chicken burger. Admittedly, it looked good, with ribbons of crispy bacon, chunks of brie cheese, and apricot sauce dripping through the layers. She'd always thought about ordering it, but the steak had won out every time. Delicious, hard to mess up, and who couldn't use a little midweek boost of iron in their diet? But she'd resolved to step outside her comfort zone so here she was, facing down the chicken burger. Though if the way Cole the Bartender had reacted when she'd ordered had been any indication, she might as well have ordered a basket of freshly slaughtered sea slugs with a side of zebra hooves. Cole, it seemed, liked change even less than Clare did.

"You gonna eat that or play with it?" he grumped at her. He'd been staring at her since setting the plate down. Clare had a sneaking suspicion there was money in the kitchen riding on whether she actually finished the meal. Wrinkling her nose at him, she picked the burger up with two hands and took a huge bite out of it. Grease and apricot sauce ran down her fingers. A tick for tidiness in the steak column, but the flavour was undeniable.

"It's delicious," she said around the hunk of bread and meat in her mouth. Or more accurately, "S'lishess". Cole didn't look convinced, but behind her the pub door opened and a blast of wintry wind ushered in another customer, so he was forced to leave her to her messy fate and go deal to the bar. She was just licking the last smear of sauce off the side of her wrist when there was a thunk and a literal god sat down across from her in the booth, grinning at her over a pint of amber beer.

"Hey there."

Clare stared at him, positive the horror coursing

through her system was readable on her face. He looked *incredible*, his new short hair highlighting the sharp lines of his face, the plush cushion of his lips, and the warmth in his dark eyes. He was wearing his three piece suit - *yum* - and a crisp white shirt, open at the neck. He looked good enough to lick, but more than that, he looked like hers.

Love, hot and visceral, rose in her throat, but she choked it back lest she vomit her affection all over him when he was just here to talk about his security deposit.

"Hello," she managed.

"What are you reading?" He nodded towards her e-reader, which was closed on the table next to her.

"Johnathon Thurston's autobiography," she answered honestly.

Manu's face, already as bright and open as the sun, softened slightly. "You are?"

"Yeah." Johnathon Thurston was a legend of rugby league. With an Indigenous Australian Gunggari and New Zealand heritage, he'd followed up an illustrious career playing league by launching an Academy for Australian youth to help develop resources for meaningful employment pathways.

"Are you enjoying it?"

"I am."

"He was a great teammate, by all accounts." Manu spoke carefully, his words hinting at a deeper meaning that she didn't have the patience to examine.

"I'm sure he was. Manu, why are you here?"

He stared at her like she'd grown a second head. "It's Tuesday. We always go to the pub on Tuesdays."

"We did," she agreed slowly. "But that was before I moved out and cried for twenty-four hours because you were insistent on putting yourself in harm's way."

Remember that, Clare? Never mind the suit. He put a game above your wishes and his health. God, that suit, though ...

He nodded slowly. "I hear you were at the game."

Clare's cheeks prickled with heat. "I was."

"With my brother."

"He invited me."

"So you know I didn't play."

Her face was on fire now. She gulped down a slug of her raspberry lemonade. Manu's beer was still untouched, and his gaze hadn't moved from her face since he sat down.

"I need your help," he announced suddenly, and she grasped at the subject change like a life raft.

"With what?" She lifted the glass to her lips again and swallowed down more of the sweet liquid.

"My family."

Her eyes narrowed. *If Aleki still managed to fuck it up after I got him here ...* "What about your family?"

"I want you to be part of it."

Her glass hit the table with a thud. The words swirled in her head and she examined them from every angle, searching for the hidden meaning to them. When she refocused, he was watching her carefully.

"Please be more specific," she croaked.

He reached out and wrapped his big, warm hands around hers. She studied them, the rich brown of his skin cupping the pale creaminess of hers, a sepia-toned photograph come to life. *Beautiful.*

"Clare," he said, and no hint of his earlier casualness existed now. "I love you. I meant it when I said it last week and I haven't changed my mind. I'm not going to change my mind." He gripped her hands tighter. "You were right, about all of it, about playing the final and who I was playing for, and I'm sorry if my actions made you believe otherwise. Six weeks ago you asked me to teach you how to be a team player, but you ended up teaching me more about teamwork than sport ever has. I want to be on your team, forever if you'll have me. I want to be your family."

She shook her head, fear flooding her body as tears dripped off her chin and onto the table. *Where did those come from?*

"It won't work," she gasped past the lump in her throat. "I love you so much, but it won't work. You're leaving. I can't be left behind again, Manu. I won't."

"I'm not leaving, sweetheart, I promise." He leaned forward pulling her closer, and the familiar smell of him was like a two-by-four to her heart. "You love me?" His eyes were gentle and shining with hope.

"Yeah." She rolled her eyes, sniffing back tears. "It's completely illogical."

A smile broke through. "Do you know what's illogical, Clare? Making the decision to stay with the Knights before they played on Saturday. Buying a ring for a girl who's never even said out loud that she likes me. Love makes us all a little illogical."

She stared at him, dazed. "What?"

"I renegotiated my contract with the Knights. I'm locked in for four years. I can't promise they won't move me on after that, but I figured it gives you enough time in your new position that you'd be able to get something similar if we had to move. Or I might be too old and broken to carry on by thirty, and we can live on your science genius salary."

"Right," she breathed, her head spinning. "And the second thing?"

A slow smile spread across Manu's face. He pulled one hand from the tangle of their fingers and reached into his suit pocket. "When you're ready, when it's *logical*, this is waiting for you." He placed a small black velvet box on the table and reached for her again, while Clare stared at the box with a mix of trepidation and desire. *Schrodinger's ring box.*

"I see. Anything else?" she asked, shooting for breezy and probably sounding asthmatic.

"Yes." Manu nodded solemnly. "I wrote an agenda."

She pulled her attention away from the ring box. "Amazing. I love it. Please continue."

Manu grinned at her and her heart soared. "There are two more items. Firstly, where to live. I would like to offer to buy Tex's apartment. It's where we met and it feels like home for us. But if you would like time to yourself, to explore other living options, please know it is your choice. Alternatively, if you would like us to get a different place together, I'm happy to do so."

She mulled it over briefly. "I like the apartment. I accept your offer to buy it. But," she said warningly, her promise to herself to stretch past the confines of her comfort zone edging her joy, "I would like to continue to live separately for another six months. I need to learn how to be my own safe space for a while."

Manu nodded briskly. "I don't like it, but I agree." He took a big breath. "Final point. Kids."

She winced instinctively, the sense of calm that had stolen over her as they negotiated shattering.

"Kids are not a dealbreaker for me." Manu's voice was gentle, his thumb skimming over the back of her hand as though calming a skittish horse. "I will never lack for children to love in my life. I have Kai and my niece on the way. And I'd be surprised if Aleki and Stella stop at one. So please know that if you never want to have kids, that is absolutely fine. I will not resent you for it. I will not leave you.

You are my family, lo'u alofa. Nothing will ever change that."

Wariness stole across Clare, pricking at her temples and accelerating her heart. "But?" *There's always a but.*

"But I think there's a chance your feelings about children may have been influenced by your experiences in your childhood and in your career. I would like to formally request that you consider discussing this with a licenced professional. This is not an ultimatum. There is no right or wrong response. It is merely a request that you think about it. Maybe you go and then start to see kids in your future, maybe you don't. No outcome will change my feelings for you. But I would like to make sure your decision doesn't come from a place of fear, when you are the strongest, most incredible person I have ever met."

She stared at Manu, at the kindness in his eyes and the waves of compassion rolling off him, as she considered his words. She turned them over in her mind, looking for loopholes. Nerves fluttered through her. Therapy had always felt like a test of sorts - *how badly screwed up are you?* - but the way he'd put it made it seem reasonable, healthy. Like something a woman finally learning how to fully understand herself might do.

Hesitantly, she raised their joined hands to her lips and pressed a kiss against his warm skin.

"That is a fair request. I accept."

Manu grinned, a brilliant slash in his handsome face. "You do?"

Clare nodded. "I do. This has been a successful negotiation."

His laugh rumbled over her, hearty and rich. "Let's make it official then. Clare Trescott, will you do me the honour of being my girlfriend and helping me negotiate my way through life next to you?"

She smiled, love and courage bursting in her chest like fireworks as she studied this man who was so dear to her. Never in her life had she imagined meeting someone who accepted her without reservations. She was almost dizzy with joy. After a lifetime of relying on herself, with only Tex to catch her on occasion, to find a teammate in Manu, someone to cheer her wins and commiserate with her on her losses, was a long-forgotten dream come true. So there was only one answer.

"No."

Panic suffused his beautiful face, and she tipped her head in the direction of the ring box, the courage he'd given her pushing the words through the curtain of fear that had filtered so many of her thoughts and words until now.

"I think, if you don't mind, I would like to be illogical now."

He arched one thick eyebrow, but he didn't hesitate. "Clare Trescott, will you do me the honour of being my wife and helping me negotiate my way through life with you?"

"I will."

She watched as he managed to deftly open the box with one hand, extract the ring and slide the band of black and white channel-set diamonds onto her ring finger, explaining how he'd forgone a high-set stone so she could wear it under her gloves at work and how the black and white had reminded him of the scientific perspective. Raising her hand to his lips, he pressed a kiss against the glittering band once it was in place before looking up at her with adoration in his eyes. Reaching over to cup his cheek, she brushed her fingers through the unfamiliar spiky velvet of his short hair.

"You like it?"

"The ring or the hair?"

"Both. Either."

"I love both."

Manu huffed out a sigh of relief. "Thank the gods." He gestured to his hair. "New beginnings." And then he rubbed his thumb over the ring on her finger. "And strong foundations. That's us."

Clare melted, the last vestiges of the wall around her heart that she'd smashed through by asking for his proposal crumbling under the tenderness of his words.

"Lo'u alofa," she murmured softly, cupping his cheek, soaking up the preciousness of the moment. "Lo'u aiga."

My love. My family.

THE END

Read on for an excerpt of *Heiress Undone,* Tex and Oliana's story!

Oliana Maiava was dying.

A tight band wound its way across her midsection, pressing against her lungs, constricting her airflow. Sweat beaded under her arms, thankfully hidden by the demure sleeves of her dress. Around her, members of her family, her *aiga*, chatted and laughed, buoyed by good food, good music and the good grace of being together in the days before Christmas. If they looked at her a little longer, a little more closely, well that was to be expected. She had been announced as the secret princess of Avali mere hours ago.

Is this how I go? A heart attack in the middle of a family reunion while they all gossip about my true parentage? Oliana sucked in another shallow lungful of air. Gods, that would be just her luck. To go toes up under the scrutiny of her entire *aiga*. The only person not shooting her inquisitive looks, in fact, was her biological father. King Tama, the man she'd thought was her uncle until three months ago, was just *there*, his ubiquitous assistant Iosefa flanking him. Her imminent demise would probably be a relief to the king - he'd barely spoken to her in the weeks since she'd discovered he'd adopted her out to his sister-in-law and her husband at birth. If not for Prince Aleki and Prince Manu discovering the truth, she might never have known.

Which might have been a blessing...

Ostensibly, this pre-Christmas family reunion was a

reception for Prince Aleki and his wife Stella, who'd broken royal protocol and more than a few hearts when they had married in secret earlier in the year. But the announcement of her royal status had changed all that. Oliana was most definitely the centre of attention and the knowledge crawled up her throat in waves of sticky discomfort.

Even knowing the announcement was coming, even with the weeks she'd had to come to terms with the news and the decades of lies of her adoptive parents, nothing could have prepared her for the feeling of being stripped bare by the eyes of her family. And found wanting.

"You look like you're thinking glum thoughts." Oliana's recently-discovered brother Manu's fiancée, Clare, flopped into the seat beside her, her grin peeping over her cocktail glass.

"Alcohol is the devil's juice," Oliana responded primly, the words of her youth flowing from her lips without hesitation. She turned back towards the party.

"Ain't that the truth. You want some?" Oliana shot a look at the curvy, dark haired woman, who waggled her eyebrows and her glass in unison. Clare had only arrived on the island last week for the first time but the feisty scientist had made quite an impact. Oliana's parents -*adoptive parents* - had had a lot to say about Manu's choice of wife and none of it positive.

That was enough to make up her mind. She held out a hand and Clare deposited the glass in it. Oliana took a quick sip, the burn of alcohol balanced by the icy tang of the mixer and the sweetness of lime.

"What is it?"

"A London Mule. Gin based. You know, the liquor of colonisers."

Oliana shot Clare a quick look as she handed the glass

back. Avali had managed to fight off the waves of British colonists sent to the Pacific until the only thing that remained was their religion, which Avalians had taken up with a vengeance.

"Interesting choice," she muttered under her breath, and Clare beamed at her.

"It is, isn't it? The way I figure it, some of the people here are going to be pissed anyway because Stella and I are *palagi* and we've wrangled your hot princes. Between Stella's secret wedding and my job undoing all of God's will regarding infertility, there's not much we can do if people are determined to dislike us. I might as well drink what I want." She sucked down another long swallow of her cocktail and handed the glass back to Oliana.

She drank again, the liquor mixing with the heat in her chest, the increased pace of her breath. Clare's words brought back the expectations of her adoptive parents as they'd prepared for her debut tonight.

'You're the last chance at keeping the royal bloodline one hundred percent Avalian.'

The thought weighed on her, pressing down on her shoulders and on the ever-shrinking hope that she might one day be able to live her own life. For twenty four years she'd been at the mercy of her parents and their demands. To be the perfect daughter, to be humble, kind and modest. She'd enrolled in university as a Psychology major after high school, only to drop out before classes started because of her father's derision and her mother's disappointment. Instead, she'd let them push her into teaching kindergarten and volunteering.

Hindsight is twenty-twenty. Obviously, they'd known this time would come, when Oliana would learn the truth about her heritage and need the skills required to survive as

Pacific royalty, but it still stung. She'd been forced into tiny boxes her whole life and if the assessing looks her family - the people who were supposed to support her - were aiming her way was any indication, it was only going to get worse when the media and general public learned about her.

"This is it." Desolation pushed the words out of her chest into the sea-scented air of the marquee.

"What is what?" Clare took back her drink.

Outside on the lawn the band stopped playing and a man's voice rang out through the speaker, but Oliana ignored it.

"My life. I'm never going to be able to be anything else. Princess Oliana. That's all I am now."

Her future sister-in-law frowned. "I don't think that's true. Look at Manu. He still gets to play sports. He has a real job as well as being a royal."

Oliana shook her head. "It's not the same. You couldn't understand." Clare had been raised in New Zealand and was unfamiliar with Avalian culture and customs.

"It's different for Manu because he's a man. The same way Avalian sons can go out with their friends but daughters require chaperones."

The traditional beliefs hadn't bothered Oliana before, but the pressure rising now under her skin threatened to explode as all the things she'd never get a chance to do ran through her mind, slide by slide, like a film filled with sound and colour and joy. Experiences that were miles from the life she'd already lived, and from the staid future that awaited her as the sole Avalian princess.

Clare leaned forward and touched her arm, but before she could speak a panicked shout echoed through the marquee.

"Call a doctor!"

A hush ran through the crowd and in the quiet that followed, a female voice spoke in English.

"Calm down, Aleki. My water broke, it's not a national emergency."

Through the press of bodies, Oliana caught a glimpse of her oldest cousin-*brother*-stalking across the wooden dance floor, pushing his pregnant wife in a wheelchair. Manu walked behind him, his phone to his ear as he scanned the room frantically.

"Oh shit," Clare muttered, and stood, hustling towards her fiancé, whose eyes lightened in relief when he saw her.

A pang of worry echoed through Oliana. Stella wasn't due until early February according to Aleki, who had mentioned it at one of the weekly meetings they'd been holding to prepare her for royal duties. But as the noise from the crowd grew and onlookers swarmed towards the entrance of the marquee, Oliana's concern for Stella faded into blissful awareness that for the first time in a very, very long time, nobody was looking at her.

So she did the one thing her body had been screaming at her to do for weeks.

She ran.

ACKNOWLEDGMENTS

My eternal gratitude to my family, who have supported me in this journey without hesitation. An extra-special shout out to my sister, who astounds me with the work she does in fertility. She answered all of my questions, even though I understood very little of what she said, and the inevitable scientific mistakes in this book are mine alone - which is probably why she won't read it.

Thanks always to Barbara De Leo for her ongoing support, guidance and assistance with all aspects of the journey. To Iona, for her keen editing eye, and the rest of my Blenheim girls for their unwavering support and pep talks.

Thank you once more to the Pacific Island community who continue to educate me and help guide me in both writing and parenting.

ALSO BY COURTNEY CLARK MICHAELS

PACIFIC PASSIONS

Royally Screwed

Heiress Undone

Christmas in Paradise

Ginger Kisses

Counting Down

Storm Warning

HOT RUGBY KNIGHTS

Game Changer

Off His Game

STANDALONES

Single Dad For The Runaway Bride

Crown Chemistry

A Pacific Passions story

By Courtney Clark Michaels

This book is a work of fiction. Names, characters, places and incidents are the product of the author's imagination or are used fictitiously. Any resemblance to persons living or dead is coincidental.

Previously published as *Rooming With Royalty*

www.courtneyclarkmichaels.com

Cover Illustration - Kerilyn Clarke

Ebook ISBN: 978-1-0670246-7-3

Print ISBN: 978-1-0670246-8-0

www.ingramcontent.com/pod-product-compliance
Lightning Source LLC
Chambersburg PA
CBHW020405210626
46816CB00006BB/2132